BEFORE THE DEVIL
KNOWS YOU'RE HERE

Sink down, Oh, traveler, on your knees,
God stands before you in these trees.

—Joseph B. Strauss

Published by Peachtree Teen
An imprint of PEACHTREE PUBLISHING COMPANY INC.
1700 Chattahoochee Avenue
Atlanta, Georgia 30318-2112
PeachtreeBooks.com

Text © 2023 by Autumn Krause
Cover image © 2023 by Michelle Avery Konczyk

Edited by Ashley Hearn
Design and composition by Lily Steele

Printed and bound in August 2023 at at Lake Book Manufacturing, Melrose Park, IL, USA.
10 9 8 7 6 5 4 3 2 1
First Edition
ISBN: 978-1-68263-647-3

Library of Congress Cataloging-in-Publication Data

Names: Krause, Autumn, author.
Title: Before the devil knows you're here / Autumn Krause.
Other titles: Before the devil knows you are here
Description: Atlanta, Georgia : Peachtree Publishing Company Inc., 2023. |
   Audience: Ages 14 and Up. | Audience: Grades 10–12. | Summary: In 1836
   Wisconsin, Catalina's determination to keep her family alive is tested
   when a bark-covered man abducts her brother, prompting her to delve into
   a world of strange beasts and tormented spirits as she uncovers the
   deep-rooted connection between her fate and the Man of Sap.
Identifiers: LCCN 2023020902 (print) | LCCN 2023020903 (ebook) | ISBN
   9781682636473 (hardcover) | ISBN 9781682636480 (ebook)
Subjects: CYAC: Magic—Fiction. | Siblings—Fiction. | Missing
   children—Fiction. | Mexican Americans—Fiction. | United
   States—History—1815–1861—Fiction. | LCGFT: Magic realist fiction. |
   Novels.
Classification: LCC PZ7.1.K7336 Be 2023 (print) | LCC PZ7.1.K7336 (ebook)
   | DDC [Fic—dc23
LC record available at https://lccn.loc.gov/2023020902
LC ebook record available at https://lccn.loc.gov/2023020903

BEFORE THE DEVIL KNOWS YOU'RE HERE

AUTUMN KRAUSE

PEACHTREE
Teen

Dedicated to my Nana, Phyllis Aratani

My first memory is with you and you led me into all
that is this life. I know, one day, I will see you again
and you will be there to lead me into the next one.
I miss you terribly. Memoria aeterna.

AUTHOR'S NOTE

I'VE ALWAYS BEEN FASCINATED BY APPLES. When I was little, I was intrigued by the seed stars nestled in their centers, imagining each apple was its own night sky. As I grew older and read more widely, I became intrigued by their literary lore. Apples are presented as Temptation, Knowledge, Beauty. They are created by gods in myths spanning different cultures, regaled as an object of Beauty in poems, depicted as the forbidden fruit in the Edenic fall in the Old Testament, and even becoming a method of poison in the famous fairy tale "Snow White." And, in America, they are wholesome icons, seen in apple pie, a gift for a teacher, and the saying, "An apple a day keeps the doctor away."

So it was from this rich landscape I got the first seeds of inspiration for *Before the Devil Knows You're Here*. I'd grown up hearing about Johnny Appleseed and always loved the idea of someone traveling far and wide, planting seeds wherever they went. But, I asked, what if Johnny wasn't planting typical apple trees? What if his apples were poisonous? Cursed?

As a triracial author, I love focusing on American history through the lens of my heritage, which is its own unique tale. My family's history is full of hope yet also full of hardship, from struggling to find the American dream while laboring in fields after emigrating from Mexico, to being wrongfully incarcerated in Japanese American internment camps during WWII. Sometimes, I get asked what it's like to be the child of interracial marriage, and I say I come from a long, proud line of it. And it's true! Despite disownment and social pressures, my direct ancestors found love and family beyond racial barriers, starting with my great-great-grandparents onward.

For this story, I told it from the point of view of a Mexican American poet, who is drawn into a surreal world full of peril. Her character is heavily inspired by my Nana, Phyllis Aratani née Comacho. Nana was a second mother to me. She was a dynamic woman with humble beginnings and spent her early childhood in the East Los Angeles Projects. At seventeen, she left high school to marry my grandpa and have her first child. But though she didn't return to formal education until she was a grandmother (funnily enough, we attended community college together, which I loved), she was a natural-born storyteller and an informal memoirist of her own story. I saw snapshots of her life as I myself grew, captured in a plethora of sticky notes to herself plastered all over her steering wheel and dashboard, beloved and humorous memories she would tell me over and over again, and in notes and dates scrawled behind countless photos in her handwriting, which is as familiar to me as her face. She was fascinated by so many things: the bodies entombed at Pompeii, sign language, old homes. When this book went on submission, she was wary of the Devil themes in it but prayed it would sell nonetheless. Sadly, she passed away before it did, but I have every confidence she knows and maybe had a hand in it.

I hope you will find her on these pages. I hope you will find something for yourself on them too. And I hope you will see the fun, wonder, and beauty that comes when you have parents from diverse backgrounds. Just beware the apples . . . they taste amazing, but I hear they kill . . .

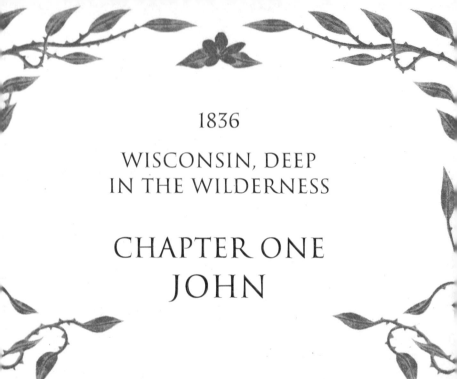

CHAPTER ONE
JOHN

MOST WOULD SAY THERE'S NO SUCH person as John Chapman. They say he died at nineteen, in the kitchen of his farmhouse. And maybe they're right. You need to have a heart to be alive and if I ever saw mine, I imagine it'd be an apple. A rotten one, sitting inside my rib cage between my lungs, putrefying me from the inside out. When I put my hand over my bark-covered chest to feel its beats, I become painfully aware of what I wish to forget:

The aphids nibbling at the leaves in my hair, making them twist and curl, though they never fall from my head.

The sticky feeling of spiders stringing their threads between my nostrils and ears.

The tickling of hundreds of ants' feet marching up and down my legs and arms.

Strongest of all is the strap on my shoulder. It's light now. The sack is nearly empty. I have sweet relief. But I've worn it for so long. I know its ways. Seeds will rise from the bottom. Their weight will make the strap pull and gouge, cutting a weeping gash in my shoulder.

I've never gotten used to the next part.

My world turns black. I'm there, eyes staring into darkness, mind awake, thoughts forming with the same slow creep of molasses oozing out of a jar. The times come closer and closer together and I know, soon, I'll be lost to them completely.

So, now, before I am lost again, I must force my hand to close around the pencil. Bark splinters at my finger joints as they bend, revealing lily-white skin underneath. It's visible only for a moment before wood grows over my knuckles and my fingers are twigs once again.

There. The pencil is in my hand, and I can begin.

I don't know if this will ever reach your eyes. But you, of all people, deserve to know my story.

I'll start long ago.

I was sixteen and dreamed of one thing: apples.

CATALINA

Three apples sat in a row on the doorstep.

Catalina saw them from the garden, where she'd been mending a hole in the fence with rope and sticks so rabbits and deer couldn't get in. The apples hadn't been there when she'd gone outside that morning, and she'd only been in the garden for about twenty minutes. No one had come bearing apples, but then no one besides Pa and Jose Luis ever came around here. Their cabin was a small island, lost against an open sea of wilderness. It was one of many that they'd lived in ever since Mamá had died. It'd been so long that Catalina's mind felt like a tool that'd been left out in the elements, its joints rusting around her thoughts so all she felt was the dull sense that, at some point long ago, there'd been words she'd wanted to say.

Wiping her hands on her skirt, she rose and squinted. The apples were still sitting in their row. Pa's voice echoed in her head.

"You die with apple on your lips, music in your ears, and his image before your eyes. . . ." It was nonsense. Lines from his fairy tales. Even so, an uneasy edge of fear cut into her. The apples were clearly placed with care. But by who? She could swear she heard something. Behind her, coming from the woods. Instinct spun her around and she stared sharply into the trees, certain that whoever had brought the apples was near, watching.

But no one was there.

She took a quick breath. There had to be an innocuous explanation for the apples. Sometimes preachers sought out families living far from town and brought them food purchased with donations from wealthy congregants back east. Her tired mind was making her conjure dangers where there were none. The hard winter had shaped her into something much more bone than blood. It was odd, though, that the apples were so beautiful. Light flowed through their dark red centers, sending splatters of sunbeams onto the threshold. She should go closer. It was too hard to see them from this distance.

"My sparrow!" Pa called to her. He'd gone out to the trapline today. She let out a small sigh of relief. Then she saw there were nothing but tiny wildflowers in his belt. He was always doing one half of a strange waltz, and today was no exception. Ambling up to her, he held out a dandelion. "A flower to gaze upon while you write."

Catalina pretended to be too busy fixing the fence to notice the dandelion.

"I don't write anymore," she said, more to herself than to him.

Before last winter, she'd written poems, scribbling them out with dirt-stained hands and pencil nubs by the fire. Jose Luis would whittle and pause to lean against her, peering over her shoulder as words danced in staccato across the page. He was her first reader, always. Didn't matter that he was also her only one. If she had a hundred readers to choose from, he would be the first. But then, slowly, she'd written less and less as the hunger had grown more and more, and she realized her brother was starving before her eyes. Finally, she'd stopped altogether, a silent bargain against the wind-driven sleet and the dwindling pantry and the skin drawing so thin around Jose Luis's face it looked like paper.

"But you must!" Pa cried, eyes owlishly magnified behind his round spectacles. His protest sparked anger in Catalina. If everyone meandered through the day as though it were a meadow, they would most certainly starve next winter. She couldn't act like him, trading in daydreams when the world traded in hunger and fear. Tying off the rope, she straightened, still ignoring the outstretched dandelion.

"There's apples," she said. "By the door."

The dandelion dropped from Pa's hand. He turned toward the cabin. Catalina watched. Long had he insisted they needed to beware apples. They were poisonous because the Man of Sap brought them. Never eat them. It certainly wasn't a hard edict to follow. Apples were a delicacy and this was the first time Catalina had directly encountered any. She placed Pa's paranoia with his stories, tales stretched tall to fit Revolutionary War haunts and St. Nicholas and La Llorona, which he retold from Mamá's canon.

Pa walked over to the apples. He stood still, staring at them. Then, without a word, he lifted his boot. It violently descended. It was rare to see him display physical strength or anger, but both twined through him. He stomped the apples, squashing. They gave easily, dark red skin turning to yellowish whiteish mush. Kneeling, he scooped the remains into a cedar bucket by the door and, without a word to Catalina, carried the remains off into the woods.

Once he was out of sight, Catalina warily went to the cabin and frowned. The apples had sat in a row like teeth on a lower jaw, waiting to snap closed. She rubbed her hand over her forehead. Whether she wanted them or not, she shared Pa's eccentricities, and she would excise them, forcing them away like her poems. At least Pa had done a thorough job sweeping up the apple slush. Nothing remained but the faintest streaks of juice.

"Guarding the door?" Jose Luis came toward her, carrying a basket. He had Pa's delicate build, one made even more frail by the previous winter. But while Pa's eyes were clouded with whims, Jose Luis's were clear, as though you could see right through to his mind. To Catalina, he seemed both young and old, the two opposite polars of life meeting in his thoughtful gaze.

"Someone has to," she said with a smile. "Come inside. I'll make us some food then come out to the field with you."

"Field." Jose Luis's countenance fell. "More like a dirt patch."

He spoke Catalina's fears aloud. Crops were necessary to survive; their paltry harvest last year—the yield of the only seeds they could afford—hadn't been enough and their pantry had emptied long before the snow melted. This year, they'd planted even fewer seeds and had no horse to plow, since Jericho had been a casualty of last winter, and no eggs because they'd been forced to eat their chickens after their food ran out. Harvest was beginning but there was hardly anything to gather. Their baskets yawned large around too-small potatoes and poorly filled ears of corn.

"Nonsense," she lied, longing to ease the worry in his face. "It's teeming with life."

Whether he believed her or not, he nodded. He set the basket down, picked up the hoe resting against the garden fence, and jousted an invisible opponent. It reminded her of the little boy she'd once ruled the woods with. In early childhood, they'd made shelters out of spiky branches and declared themselves king and queen of the magical woodland. They'd run over the open fields with bare legs and untamed hair, screaming at the top of their lungs for the sheer pleasure of the wild sound. They'd fought invisible armies of pirates or soldiers or ghosts, side by side. That wildling creature inside Catalina had died, time and loss drawing her into adulthood after Mamá was gone and they moved time and again, but she was determined to keep it alive in Jose Luis— and to keep him alive, period.

Seemingly successful in his joust, Jose Luis set the hoe against the cabin and went inside. Catalina began to head after him but stopped at the doorway. Bending down, she stared. The apple's juice had turned sludgy. A revolting smell rose from the streaks, one laced with musty, wet rot. How could that be? The apples had been in the peak of health. Alarmed, she kicked dirt over it.

Then she hurried into their cabin, though the putrid scent trailed after her, as though following her inside.

Pa didn't come home till supper, but that wasn't uncommon. He often was in the throes of projects soon to be abandoned: digging a channel from the stream to their field, building newfangled snares, constructing a smokehouse. All good ideas if they'd ever be completed and if there weren't more pressing things to do. Catalina was the one who made certain the tasks for their survival got ticked off, one by one.

Gruffly, Pa sat down at the table, face cut from unrelenting stone until they made the sign of the cross over themselves. It was a gesture Mamá used to do all the time. When she was worried. When she was happy. When she was tucking Catalina and Jose Luis in bed—only then she made it over them, as though it were a blanket for them to settle beneath.

"After supper," Catalina said, noticing Jose Luis watching Pa with worry, "we should read some Sor Juana."

Sor Juana de la Cruz was Mamá's favorite poet. Mamá had owned a book of her poems—poemas, as she called them—and translated every one of them with a pencil so they could practice reading. The book was on the mantel, which they'd turned into an ofrenda displaying the treasures Mamá had brought with her from Mexico. Her mantilla veil, folded and wrapped in cloth, sat next to her two red glass candleholders. The candles had long ago burned down to stubs. The sight hurt Catalina's heart. They only used the fire for light now, having no time or animal fat to render into tallow for new candles. It seemed wrong. Flames were immediate and present, and whenever Catalina lit them for Mamá, she seemed more immediate and present too, as though the flickering shadows from the bobbing flames were cast there by her skirts as she moved through the cabin.

Pa poured water from their pitcher into his cup and took a long swig. He set it down with a clatter. Catalina stifled a sigh. Once he was in a bad mood, it was hard to get him out of it. She wished she could ask him about the apples, but it would drive him further into the quicksand of his thoughts. It would be better to keep talking to Jose Luis instead.

"Which poem—*Pa?*" Pa's hands scrabbled at his throat, as though trying to claw out the water he'd drank. Behind his spectacles, his eyes were so wide they were nearly all whites, the pupils swiveling around for help. Catalina jumped to her feet, knocking her chair over. Jose Luis stared in horror. "What's wrong? Pa!"

He started to get up but fell forward onto the table, crashing into the dishes and knocking over the pitcher. Water gushed out. A bubbly red foam swirled through the liquid. The fragrance of apples blended with a vile, corrosive odor. Catalina grabbed Pa and tried to lift him. What had been in the pitcher?

"Jose Luis! Help!" Catalina screamed. Face white, Jose Luis hurried over to support him. Even though Pa was a small man, he fell through their hands, dragging all three of them to the floor in a grotesque family portrait. His head lolled back in Catalina's lap. "Get up. We need to get him to the bed."

Together, they hoisted him onto his bed. Catalina tried to figure out what was wrong, what had happened. Red marks spread out from his mouth and down his neck, following the path of the water. When she pulled open his shirt, the marks webbed to the center of his chest, where they then shot out, multiple prongs of one lurid star.

There were only remedies to try. She put wet washcloths on his forehead, dosed him with tonic from the bottle, made a poultice of gum salve. Jose Luis aided, but eventually she told him to go to sleep.

Nothing worked, and as the night cupped a hand over the cabin, darkness penetrated their home.

CHAPTER TWO
CATALINA

PA LINGERED FOR TWO DAYS. AS THE HOURS slipped by and night fell on the second day, exhaustion lulled Catalina into a soporific daze. Chill settled in the cabin, the first harbinger of fall so she'd bundled herself. Pa's jacket hung off her shoulders and the green and yellow jorongo Mamá had woven for Pa brushed her knees. She clutched both, curled into them. A remote part of her mind repeated lines from *The First Dream*, one of Sor Juana's poems. Usually Sor Juana's poems sprang from the earth of Catalina's mind, blooming flowerlike, full of life. Now, the petals wilted, singed by the sense of grief to come.

Dead to life
Alive to death.

Soon, lines from her own poems wandered through her thoughts, her old self's ghost coming to haunt her. She was too tired to force them away.

Fire flickers across my page,
lines of alternating bright and dark,
and I don't know if it is light to see by
or shadows to steal my thoughts away.
And so I

Her poem ended there and, upon reaching its unfinished end, it began again in her mind, unwieldy and confused.

"Catalina." Jose Luis's hand was warm on her shoulder. "Sleep. You must sleep and let me take a turn."

"No." Dry, cracked lips made it hard to speak. "I don't need to."

"Go. Now." Rarely did Jose Luis assert himself and Catalina was so tired, she nodded. Though her mind was heavy, her body seemed to float to the bed. Sleep claimed her before she fully closed her eyes.

Catalina woke with a gasp. She was sitting, though she had no memory of pushing herself up. Her hand was in the pocket of Pa's jacket, though she had no memory of that either. Foggy gray morning light slanted into the cabin through the greased paper covering the window.

Something cold looped around her fingers in her pocket. It was one of the temples of Pa's spectacles. She'd taken them off as he thrashed. The memory made her stomach turn, sending a wave of sick through her. She snatched her hand back.

Numbly, she got up and dragged herself to where Jose Luis sat in a chair next to Pa's bed.

"You let me sleep too long," she whispered. "How is he?"

"I—I don't think he's good." Jose Luis looked gravely up at her, as though he knew something she didn't yet. Catalina peered down at Pa. Her breath snagged cruelly in her throat. Mamá had died a different sort of death. She'd been mauled by a bear just out of hibernation, not taken by whatever poison coursed through Pa. But the look of death on Mamá's face hovered close to Pa's, as though it simply needed the gentlest push to descend and settle on him. Earlier, he'd tossed and turned and spoke in English and broken Spanish. Now, he was motionless. His face was a ghoulish gray and it almost seemed as though he were made of wax.

"Go rest. I'll watch him," she said firmly. Jose Luis got up and threw himself onto his bed. He turned to the wall. Catalina took Pa's hand. As always, his nails were clean and carefully shaped and though calluses toughened his palm, softness was under it. She held it, tight, willing the hardness and strength of her hand into his so he could take it and fight this poison. If only such trades could be made.

Pa's mouth slipped open. A watery, high note wound through his breath. The red patchwork over his mouth, neck, and chest had spread, covering his face and torso and reaching down his arms. Eyes glittering with fever shone between wispy lashes. Catalina leaned over.

"Pa?" she asked. "Can you hear me?"

No recognition lit his eyes. He needed his spectacles. That was the answer. She stuck her hand in her pocket, pulled them out, and extended the ear loops. Then she stopped.

Pa's eyes were still open, but the lids hung limply over them, like curtains waiting to be drawn. Death had descended.

She understood it in an instant, yet her mind rejected the knowing. Her hand, as though determined to finish its task, lifted to still put his glasses on. His last vision of the world couldn't be a blurry wash of shapes. Pa's eyesight was so terrible he couldn't even read a book without his glasses. But it was too late. He would never read again. He would never see again. He would never offer her another dandelion.

Grief sank into her heart, into her marrow. She sat back, staring at Pa. Early morning sunlight pried through the cracks in the cabin's caulking by the bed and fell across him. Small daubs of light rested over his face, circles glowing on his skin as though his soul leaked through them. A hot pearl of sweat ran down the side of Catalina's face and she thought it was a tear. That would be best, to cry for Pa. She returned his spectacles to her pocket.

The door tore away. With a scream, Catalina jumped to her feet. Wind burst through the cabin like a ferocious intruder storming into their home. It sent a vertical hail of dirt, twigs, and leaves through the room. It knocked over their table and chairs and flung back the quilt draped over Pa. Jose Luis lunged to his feet, but a piece of firewood, tossed as easily as a matchstick, struck his head. He collapsed to the floor.

Someone was framed in the door. No, *something*. She saw a head, shoulders, arms, legs—the usual accoutrements of humanity—but—but—Catalina's eyes widened.

It was a man, but his skin rose and fell in patchy, lopsided ridges. *Bark?* Green leaves with serrated edges sprouted from his hair. Birds circled his head. Red birds with talons tipped in claws, the claws curved as though waiting to lock around prey like a cage. A burlap seed sack hung from his shoulder and a rusted pot sat on his head.

His gaze penetrated the room. The eyes were covered in a thick substance. It oozed down his cheeks in slow yellow tears that built into a crust around his chin.

Catalina wanted to shake Jose Luis awake and run. Run with every bit of her might until they were safe deep in the woods. But she knew better. You didn't run in the wilderness. Running made things chase you, chase you until they caught and devoured you. When starving wolves circled the cabin last winter, Pa lit a torch and gave Catalina a pan to bang from the safety of the cabin. He'd yelled and hooted and scared the mangy creatures off. Then, when a brown bear and her cubs caught them unawares by the river, he'd had them pretend to be dead.

Scream or play dead.

Wolf or bear?

Or . . . human?

"Who are you?"

Her voice was raspy with fear, her heart a rabid jackrabbit in her chest. She stared at his barky skin and leafy hair, her mind spinning away from a single name.

The Man of Sap.

She heard the line in her head, spoken in Pa's theatrical yet unsettled tone.

Sowing seeds of sin, he grows apples of ash.

The character from Pa's story. He was alive. He was standing here, in front of her, in their cabin.

"You're the Man of Sap." The words fell from Catalina's mouth in a tremulous gasp, and the birds around his head cawed as though to herald his name. His eyes lit behind the goopy tears.

"John, actually." His lips peeled back, showing improbably white teeth. "Answer me, quickly. Are you Catalina Josefina? Is that Jose Luis?"

He took a step toward her brother, who still lay slumped on the floor. Light-headedness rushed over Catalina. She had to fight. She had to stop him before he reached Jose Luis. Pa's rifle had been knocked off the wall and was too far to reach. But their shovel was nearby, its scoop rusty but sharp.

She dove for it, her body moving with a swiftness she didn't know it possessed. Her knees hit the floor. Twin pains shot through them. She grasped the shovel.

Instantly, he was right there, upon her.

With equal speed, she rose. Swung the shovel. The scoop sliced through the air. Blade chopped through wood. But it wasn't wood. It was his wrist, *his hand*. A scream of horror ripped from her. John screamed too. His blood spurted across her face. No, not blood. Sap. Some got in her mouth, the bizarre, subtle taste of sweetness spreading across her tongue.

John lifted his arm and, right before her eyes, the stump sprouted. Regenerated. Knobby buds hardened over it and burst into blooms and then leaves. Human bone grew from the protrusion, building into a wrist and then separating into fingers. Veins, muscles, and sinewy tendons wormed across the bones, latching and securing themselves to it. Finally, skin, flushed with newness, unrolled over it all. It was there. A hand, as whole and hale as could be. It compulsively opened and closed. He brought it to his face and stared with awe. Then texture spread across the skin. Bark. It rose at bumpy angles, breaking through the fresh, delicate flesh and enclosing it entirely.

What was this impossible magic? The question shook her, but she couldn't think. Not now. She had to move while he was distracted. Swinging the shovel again, she aimed for his head. The birds saw the motion before he did and shrieked in warning. He ducked at the last moment. Uselessly, the shovel sliced through the air.

One of his birds flew at her. Wings beat mercilessly against her face, and talons dug into her skin. Blindly, she struggled forward, unable to see beyond the flapping barrage. The edge of a loose plank caught her foot and she sprawled to the floor. Blood filled her mouth. Dully, she realized she'd bitten her tongue. Something sharp gouged her thigh. Pa's spectacles in her pocket. The shards of glass cut through her skirt and into her leg. The bird cawed victoriously over her.

She jumped up. John had grabbed Jose Luis and hoisted him over his shoulder. Her brother stirred but didn't awaken. She held up her hands.

"I'll give you anything. Please, just let him go." Catalina took a tentative step forward. "Tell me what you want."

John's lips parted to speak, but a ripple spread out. It was a movement in the air, like steam across glass or a breeze across water. It filled the cabin and the same wind as before whipped up into a frenzy, blasting her back. The birds settled onto John's shoulders and the pot on his head, their talons scratching loudly against its metallic bottom. John spoke but the sound was drowned out by the howling gale. Impulse dictated that Catalina close her eyes and hold up her hands to protect her face from the hail of twigs, dirt, and leaves that rained down on her. But she didn't. Nothing could make her take her gaze off her brother, even as dust stung her eyes.

She saw John take a step toward her as though trying to grab her as well. She should take a step back to protect herself. Instead, she threw herself forward at them. Whatever was happening, she would stop it. But the wind was a whirlpool of force and she spun off it, hitting the floor once again.

They disappeared.

Catalina screamed her brother's name as the world calmed. The wind bumbled about itself, tumbling in little fitful bursts before dissolving. No one answered her. There was nothing but emptiness, so complete that it seemed lunacy to think that John and her brother had been there, only moments ago. She sank to her knees, eyes caught in a ceaseless flutter between the door and where John had stood with Jose Luis, as though they could reconfigure what they'd just seen. Her brother had been snatched through the fabric of reality by a monster from a tale. A monster who had known her name, who'd seemed to recognize Pa.

She wavered on the sharp pinpoint of despair, the sort that could end you right where you stood. Then she forced herself to stand. There had to be clues. When an animal moved through the woods, it left a chain of prints, clumps of fur on low-hanging branches, scratch marks on mossy trees. Everything left something behind, all the world testifying about its own existence.

But she had to do something else first. She went to Pa. Her hands trembled as she fumbled to cross Pa's hands on his chest. They trembled even more as she tried to close his eyelids. No matter what she did, they wouldn't stay shut. The bottom curve of his pupils hung beneath the lids. Finally, she gave up and picked up the quilt that had been blown onto the floor and tucked it over him. She pulled it to his chin and then, taking a breath that she didn't feel, lifted it over his face.

Task complete, she turned, forcing her mind to sharpen, even as grief for Pa wrung from her as though she were a twisted, wet dishrag. The cabin door had been blown off its hinges and tossed aside, as though it was no heavier than dandelion fluff. She ran outside, circled their home. But there were no tracks. Not a single footprint was left in the dirt. It was as though John had dropped on their doorstep out of nowhere.

Madness. This was madness. She went back inside and righted the chair where she'd held vigil next to Pa. Sinking into it, she sat by Pa's body, recalling what he had said about the Man of Sap.

He's evil itself. He walks the earth with his sack of seeds, and plants them wherever he can. They become apple trees, bearing the reddest and juiciest fruit you've ever seen. They call to you. They don't speak aloud but they whisper to your soul. Take a bite and they're the best thing you've ever eaten. And the last. He watches while you die, and his birds sing a song. Normally, those birds sound mighty ferocious but, as you fade, they sound sweet. You die with apple on your lips, music in your ears, and his image before your eyes.

None of it helped. She had to think. Harder. After a few more minutes, she stood. He needed a grave and she needed an answer. Maybe it would come to her as she laid him to rest.

There was a hole out back. Pa had dug it, declaring he'd found just the spot for a well and that Catalina wouldn't have to draw water from the river again. It was another plan he shortly gave up, but the hole was deep and wide enough. Little had he known that he'd dug his own grave.

Fetching their ancient wheelbarrow, she maneuvered it to the bedside and tipped Pa's body into it. The wheelbarrow rattled and screeched as she pushed it to the hole, making her ears ring. Pa's limbs bounced about in front of her as she jerked it over the uneven dirt. She tried to ease his body gently into the hole, but it was unceremonious and cruel. His body flopped into it. Carefully, she draped the quilt over him once again and filled the hole with their shovel. John's sap stained its edge. She tried to think, to plan, even as she buried Pa.

A fluttering of red wings caught her eye, and she paused mid-shovel. One of John's birds settled on the ground near the grave. Its beady eyes blinked at her. Pa's words echoed in her mind once more: *The birds follow him.*

With a ruffling of its wings, the bird marched toward Catalina. It looked her up and down and bobbed its head. If Pa was right, it would go back to John. The bird knew the way, a compass was embedded deep inside it, the sort that returned salmon to their old nests after a year away.

Should she follow it?

Still holding the shovel aloft, she stared at the bird. It was about the size of a robin, but its wings were tipped in sharp points and blades protruded from its back. It seemed more weapon than bird, as though sinister intent lay behind its design, one that went far beyond flight and feathers.

But she had no other choice. John left no trail.

For now, her only option was to follow it, so she would. She would track it to John. And then she would kill him and save her brother.

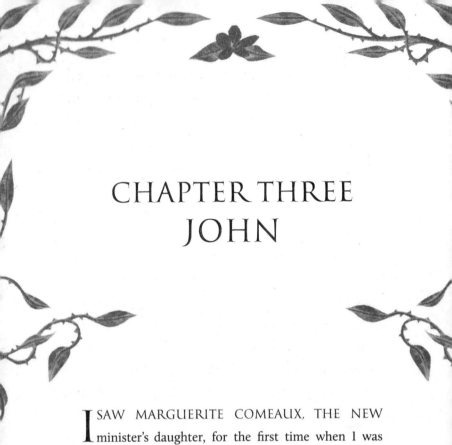

CHAPTER THREE
JOHN

I SAW MARGUERITE COMEAUX, THE NEW minister's daughter, for the first time when I was sixteen. Rosiness blossomed across her cheeks, and she wore a bright red dress as she walked through town, a basket on her arm. She reminded me of an apple, and I was drawn to her like a fruit fly. Unfortunately, so were the other fellows. They brought her flowers, but I wanted to give her something better. My father, when he was in town and sober enough to walk a straight line, would bring me an apple. He'd shine it on his sleeve until it seemed to glow. "There's a whole galaxy in here, boy," he'd say, cutting it in half to reveal the star made from seeds sitting at its center. "And a star just for you." I wanted to give her one too. To me, there was no finer gift. But the town was short on fruit shipments, and the only apple tree belonged to the mercantile owner. Though he sold most things, he kept the apples solely for himself. He did, however, sell seeds.

All I wanted was to approach her, but my courage faltered. I was always a loner, a boy with hair falling into his eyes and a drunk father who came and went, subject to the golden tides of whiskey. Girls whispered around me, and I realized they thought I was handsome. It was a horrifying thought. I didn't have any friends, much less paramours. I started walking through town quickly, with my head down, avoiding girls as though they were puddles. But when I saw Marguerite, my tightly closed heart wondered what it would be like to open, just a little. Lord knew it was ridiculous to even hope she might like me, given she was the minister's daughter, and I was the son of a drunken devil.

I decided to talk to her at the corn husking, but my courage failed. Fellow after fellow approached her, one sitting next to her during the husking, one escorting her to the punch bowl, and yet another whirling her around the dance floor after the corn had been shucked. I left the barn to stand outside. There was a flask in my pocket. I loathed and longed for it, feeling the haunt of my father upon me. The struggle didn't last long. I took it out and drank deeply.

Just as I did, Marguerite appeared by my side like a beatific vision. The unexpected sight of her made me choke. I tried to hold straight and stifle the coughing, but it only made my eyes stream tears and the hacking worse. Mortified, I turned away. She grinned, her red dress looking black in the night, and held out her hand for the flask. Bashfully, I handed it to her, and she took a swig herself without so much as wincing.

"Tabarnak, that's good!" she laughed, not sounding like a minister's daughter at all. "Now, ask me to dance, mon cheri."

It was like dancing with a sunbeam, the warmth of her melting away the cold that had long settled inside me. I was stiff and wooden, but she seemed lighter than air. Later that night, when we said goodbye, I told her I had something for her. I dipped my hand into my pocket and turned to her. Her eyes were closed, and her lips puckered. She'd thought I meant a kiss. I froze. I'd never kissed anyone before. I'd never gotten close enough to anyone to even consider it. Blood thundered in my ears. Everything in me wished to grab her and kiss her. But if I did, she might see right through me, as though I were a pane of glass, and know I didn't deserve her light. One of her eyes winked open to see what the delay was, and then she opened both.

"Oh!" she giggled. "You meant something real."

"Yes . . . I . . ." My tongue was unwieldy in my mouth. Finally, face blazing with embarrassment, I held out her gift.

"What is that?" She squinted in the moonlight. "A seed?"

"An apple seed," I mumbled, feeling odious and stupid.

Eagerly, she snatched it from my hand and pinched it between her thumb and pointer fingers.

"Why, it looks just like a jewel," she said. "How remarkable that an entire tree will grow from something so teeny tiny."

"It is remarkable," I agreed. "And that tree will live for generations, bearing apples not only to the person who plants it but to their descendants as well."

"What I wouldn't give for a juicy apple right now," Marguerite sighed.

I said, "I have a plan. To plant a commercial orchard, so the apples can be enjoyed by everyone, not just the family who owns it."

"How delightful! You must do it."

She spoke so easily, as though she could already see my vision. No one had ever expressed confidence in me before. My heart lifted, slipping free from the heavy doubts always tethering it to the real world. I pulled her close and kissed her, losing myself to her soft lips and soft hands.

Marguerite had called my gift something real but, in that moment, I learned there's more to realness than something you can touch. Our kiss couldn't be held or passed from hand to hand, but it was the realest thing I'd ever experienced. If I close my eyes and think on it long enough, it still makes me smile, even after all this time. Even after all I've done.

We wed six months later, despite her father's disapproval. Marguerite wore her bright red gown with matching ribbons in her hair, and I snagged an apple from the merchant's yard to give to her that night. She wanted to honeymoon in Québec to show me where she grew up, but I told her I had a surprise planned. So off we went to Myers, Michigan.

"What shall we do today?" Marguerite asked, lounging in our hotel room and woefully surveying a flyer advertising a sing-along at a local church, the only event happening that whole week. "There are so many things to pick from," she said dryly. "How shall we ever decide?"

"I know this isn't the most glamorous place," I said. "But I promise it will all be worth it. I have a quick errand to run."

"For my surprise?" She brightened. I'd come to learn she loved surprises, and it made me want to fill her life with them. "What are you up to? Tell me, I can't bear it—no, don't tell me!"

"You know me, my little sun," I said, bending to kiss her. "I'm always trying to do something."

"It's true. You are clever and formidable. Don't let anyone tell you otherwise, mon cheri."

I headed off, steps galvanized with optimism. Wisconsin was part of Michigan Territory back then, and I heard Governor Hull and his administration were working with farmers to establish a horticultural society. I'd made an appointment to meet with the governor and his board to propose the idea of a trial apple orchard funded by the government. As I walked into the meeting, I imagined my future family with Marguerite and how I would give my children apples, just as my father did when he was in town. I couldn't wait to see Marguerite's eyes shine when I went back to the hotel and revealed exactly why we'd come here.

Standing before the board who were stuffily attired in fancy black suits and ruffled neckerchiefs, I described my vision: apples, cultivated for everyone, nourishing the whole state inside out. Those men looked at each other and shook their heads.

"The growing season is too short here," one said.

"And the winters are much too harsh for a commercial apple orchard," another added.

"It's true," I said. "But apples are hardy. I just need to plant the right ones. Maybe even create new breeds, ones that will ripen quickly ahead of the frost."

But the men, each one an identical copy of the other, had their noses so high in the air that they couldn't see beyond them, much less beyond the confines of established agriculture. Marguerite's words, the ones that had encouraged me just that morning, turned against me. Clever and formidable. They thought I was a joke. I resolved to make them see, no matter the cost.

Heading back to the hotel with no surprise for Marguerite was the longest walk of my life. I poured everything out to her once I got there, my head cradled in her lap. She stroked my forehead and shook her head and cursed those men in French. After I'd let her down, all she cared about was making me feel better.

Someday, I vowed silently, I would give her an apple and show her the star inside. A star for my sun. I would make it happen, no matter what.

By the time I was eighteen, I was a husband of almost two years and a father for one year to a son, Gabriel. Thoughts of an apple orchard loomed every time I closed my eyes to sleep, but life was sweet and happy. Despite long hours at the mill, I always came home to joyful faces and sometimes I thought I might just let the apple orchard vision go and that I would be all right without it.

Then Marguerite suffered a grave blow. Both her parents died during the typhoid epidemic. She grew wan, the bright light always so easily shining from her dimmed by these new clouds.

She drew her shawl tight to her chest and her father's Bible even tighter. I held her, wishing I could take away her pain. I was made for pain. She was not. I saw her become scared of the world's vicissitudes, those fluctuating waters I'd been born into and swum through my entire life.

The deaths meant she received a large inheritance. I knew what to do. She needed a distraction. She needed to witness the miracle of apples growing before her eyes to restore her lost light.

I scouted near and far throughout our region of Wisconsin and found an apple orchard for sale. Walking through it, I knew I'd found my Eden. A determination came over me, so strong it felt like I was drunk. No matter what, I had to have that orchard.

Marguerite, though I told her it would make her happy again, only saw the risk. What if the orchard failed to yield? What if I couldn't figure out how to distribute the apples commercially? I didn't have much experience as a farmer—what if I couldn't figure out how to tend the trees? I couldn't blame her. It *was* risky to purchase it, leave my job at the mill, and sink everything we had into the venture. Secretly, I wondered if my father's nature was upon me, driving me to an ill end. He never found the bottom of a bottle, or the end of a poker game. Risk. Reward. Loss. The endless cycle had defined his life and his death at the hands of a man he'd owed money. It was like his spirit had nowhere to go, so it returned to me, whispering in my ear to follow my own will, no matter the consequences.

Canker struck just on the cusp of my first harvest. I did what I could to save my trees. Carefully cut out lesions from the trunks, wincing as the knife sliced deep. By the time it was over, my trees were pockmarked in gouges, the delicate, pink innards of the wood beneath their bark exposed. It didn't seem right that healing would come from such hurt.

"I'm sorry," I whispered to the trees. "I'm sorry," I said again, later that night to Marguerite over dinner. "Don't worry. The trees will heal and prosper."

She pushed her chair back. I think it was because the baby was fussing. Or maybe it was already forming. The rift that would grow so wide between us that eventually no manner of bridge could cross it. And who could blame her? I convinced her to wager all our—all *her*—savings on this orchard. Instead of lifting her out of her darkness, it plunged her deeper.

Despite my efforts, the canker won. There wasn't a single apple to harvest that year.

❧

CATALINA

Catalina needed supplies. Quickly. The bird could take off at any moment. She turned her last shovelful of dirt over Pa's grave. It wasn't fully filled in, but he was covered. No hints of the quilt peeked through the mound. She set the shovel aside and hovered like a worried butterfly. There were prayers to say. Words of remembrance. A cross to make and stake into the ground to declare that there had been a man and that he now slept here, beneath the dirt. Only there was no time.

Running to the cabin, she thought of Pa. Not as she had for the past recent years, but rather as she had when she was little, when her pa was the person who could make everything right. He had seemed made from a tale himself, a soul belonging in a storybook of wonder and whimsy. Sometimes, he would toss her into the sky, his eyes twinkling as though he thought he might just see her fly.

The memory whittled against her bones, weakening her. She forced it aside. That was the thing about grief. She had learned it when Mamá died: it would always be there, waiting. It was water seeping through every barrier you erected to hold it back, every patch in the wall, every board nailed in place. It was quick to seep and even quicker to rise. Whether you could keep it at bay long enough to survive was up to you. And she would, for Jose Luis. She picked up Pa's rifle, ready to sling it over her shoulder. It was bent in half from being blasted off the wall by John's storm. No good. Pa's hunting knife. It lay on the ground in its leather sheath. She snatched it.

It was much heavier than she'd anticipated. It had a fixed blade and a wood handle, carved for Pa's grip, not hers. It was meant for piercing, skinning, or slicing—once an animal was dead. If you used it in defense, its short handle meant the animal was already upon you. The knife was awkward in her grasp. She'd chopped John's hand off and it'd grown right back. What was a knife against such a being? Hell, what was a girl like herself against him?

No. She was a child of the wilderness and though it was a brutal mother, it had taught her well. Every creature had its weakness. She'd seen the ravaged body of a bear torn apart by a wolf pack and the remains of a rabbit slain by an ermine half its size. There was a way to kill John. She just had to figure it out.

Into the sheath went Pa's knife and she dropped it into a satchel. Put jerky into the satchel, filled a canteen with water from the bucket, and put that in too. Rope. Matches. Wool blanket. Even though the weather was fair, she left on Pa's jacket and the jorongo Mamá had woven. They would keep off the chill at night. And they made her feel stronger, like she was a girl walking alongside ghosts who wished to protect her.

The bird cawed from the door and flew around the cabin in a low circle. Catalina ducked as its talons nearly caught her hair. She went to the items that had been cast off the mantel. Hands gentle, she replaced the bundle of cloth holding Mamá's wedding mantilla. Sor Juana's book of poetry had landed facedown. The spine looked like a stem from which the open cover and pages grew. It wouldn't be wise to take it into the woods. But a reckless need made her reach for it, and she snatched it up with the sort of desperation you grab medicine when sick or food when starving.

Another caw came as the bird dove toward the door. Catalina put the book in the satchel and followed it.

The bird plunged straight into the woods and Catalina hurried after it. It paused every now and again on branches before flitting onward and she struggled to keep up. Late summer rains had fattened the wilderness, making it full and dense, as though it wore a coat it had made for itself. Fall had begun to daub the woods like an artist sampling out ochres, ambers, and vermilions. Its beauty was a warning for Catalina. When the trees donned their gold autumnal crowns, it meant winter was circling, waiting to turn the trees to skeletons and the world to ice.

Their cabin faced a path that led to a road. That road eventually led to town. Civilization. Woods encroached on the back of their cabin, woods that went on for miles upon miles. The US government had steadily pushed the Menominee, Chippewa, Potawatomi, and Ho-Chunk out, sometimes even giving the stolen land to European immigrants for free. Catalina's family used to live in the Green Bay settlement but after Mamá died, Pa seemed to flee from both life and the government, which sought farmers to take the land. He plunged them into the woods, squatting, erecting ramshackle cabins, and moving before anyone could figure out they were there. They'd lived in this last cabin for only a year. Catalina was familiar with the first few acres where their trapline ran near the forking streams, but after that . . . it was as mysterious as the far reaches of the night sky. She was being pulled further and further from the known.

This was a new isolation. It settled around Catalina like a high level of altitude, making it hard to breathe. There was no getting used to it. When they lived in the settlement, she and Jose Luis had attended class in the clapboard one-room schoolhouse. The teachers were stern figures who doled out punishment from their rulers, but the stories she learned were hers to keep, always. After Mamá died and they began moving from one plot in the wilderness to the next, though Catalina hadn't realized it at the time, she'd already begun to set aside her words, putting them into a drawer of her mind and closing it.

Eventually, Pa took them on one of his long sojourns to town, and Catalina witnessed how things had changed. There were many more European settlers. Tension filled it, as the United States broke treaties with tribal governments and battles raged between the two. Traders carried with them rumblings of other troubles, embodied in heated debates about relations between Mexico and the United States.

On that trip, a European man had overheard Catalina and Jose Luis playing and calling each other by name. He stared at them, taking in their dark hair and eyes, inheritances from Mamá—heirlooms, in Catalina's opinion—then he looked to Pa, who had blond hair, blue eyes, and pinky-white skin that was much lighter than theirs. Sidling up to them, he said Texas belonged to the United States of America and followed it with something derogatory about a white man having children with a woman from Mexico.

Pa's eyes, which were always so dreamy and distant, filled with fury and he sputtered. The man laughed and walked away, until Pa finally found his voice and yelled, "You're a small-minded knave. Marrying their mother was the only right thing I ever did in my life" but only Catalina and Jose Luis heard him.

The disgust in the man's voice angered Catalina. People, she realized, were their own type of wilderness, just as cruel, just as unpredictable, just as powerful. She was grateful for Jose Luis. Their siblinghood was a hallowed bond that held their hopes and fears in common accord. Whatever happened to one, they vowed, would happen to the other. Until now.

A root made Catalina stumble and the bird paused, glancing back at her. Bristling, she demanded, "What're you looking at?"

It was nice to hear a human voice, even if it was her own. She wasn't used to walking through the woods without Jose Luis. While she regarded the red bird with caution and fear, he would likely see it with interest. He always had unexpected reactions to things. Last winter, he had found a baby mouse with a broken leg just before the first big snowfall. The merciful thing would've been to snap its neck. Put it out of its misery. There was no way it would survive the winter. That was the thing about life in the wilderness: cruelty and kindness were often the same.

But Jose Luis whittled a tiny splint, and painstakingly tore strips of muslin off their cheesecloth to tie the splint onto the mouse's leg. The mouse was barely old enough to eat food and they didn't have any to give. Frustrated, she told Jose Luis not to feed the mouse because he needed sustenance himself. Time and again, though, she found him hand-feeding crumbs into the mouse's pink, eager mouth.

"Stop feeding it!" she demanded as they huddled near the embers of the fireplace. "Tell him, Pa."

But Pa said dreamily, "Perhaps the mouse is a king. We shan't keep food from the king."

Exasperated, she turned her back on Pa and repeated to Jose Luis, "Don't waste food on a mouse."

"But I found him," he said evenly.

"So? There are hurt animals in the woods every day."

"I was thinking about how hungry I was, and I found him. I was hungry, but he was hungry and hurt."

"Then maybe you should've eaten him."

Jose Luis smiled, and Catalina was pleased to see it, despite her frustration.

"I'm not keen on roasted mouse," was all he said.

Somehow, the four of them made it through the winter.

Night set upon them. The sun plummeted fast, as though a weight drew it to the earth's other side. Thick shadows sprang up between the trees and plants. John's bird sensed the turning of the day. It stopped on a high branch and snuggled against the trunk, roosting.

"No!" Catalina called out. "Keep going."

With a ruffling of feathers, the bird pulled closer to the trunk, ignoring her.

"Please. Please, keep going."

Its only reaction was to tuck its head under its wing. There would be no more travel tonight. For a moment, she turned in a circle, part of her tempted to plunge on in the direction they'd been heading. But there was no path to follow. The bird was both her path and map.

She would make camp. Continue tomorrow.

Dejectedly, she cleared a small area near the base of the tree. The air was cold, tinged with the first breaths of the coming fall. Gathering dead leaves, she arranged them in a loose pile and then steepled fallen branches over them. She lit a match and held it to the pile of leaves. It warily nipped at the leaves and then bit, the flame eating through the brittle leaves and greedily fanning out to the branches for more. She sat with her back to the trunk.

The sounds of the nighttime ran wild around her, making the cabin seem like a faraway dream. She tried to focus on the deep hoots of the owls and the calls of the nighthawks and not the baying of wolves. Even more so, she tried to force away the haunting image of Pa lying dead in the bed. She reached into the satchel and pulled out the poetry book. It was too dark to see but she held it and, closing her eyes, recited one of Sor Juana's poems, "In Which She Satisfies a Fear with the Rhetoric of Tears," in her head.

Amid my tears that were poured out by pain,

my heart became distilled, was broken through.

The rawness of the poem spoke to her, captured in words like *poured out*, *distilled*, and *broken through*. Sor Juana had died long ago—she'd been a poet nun in New Spain—but her words were alive, undimmed in their passion, and, somehow, they made her feel less alone.

Clearing her throat, she let herself recall her own unfinished poem. Maybe if she said it aloud, it would be like talking to Sor Juana in their shared language of poetry—like she was here.

In a wavering voice, Catalina said,

"Fire flickers across my page,

lines of alternating bright and dark,

and I don't know if it is light to see by

or shadows to steal my thoughts away.

And so I . . ."

Just as it always did, the poem stopped. Incomplete. She could try to finish it as she waited for sleep, but when she tried to think of the next lines, anger flared in her chest. Here she was. Alone. No poem said or unsaid could help.

There was a rustling in the tree above her and she glanced up. The bird had pulled its head out from under its wing, listening. It waited, as though wanting her to finish the poem and, when she didn't, tucked back against the tree and slept.

CHAPTER FOUR
CATALINA

CATALINA WOKE AT DAWN WITH A START. Somehow, she'd slept and the fire was smoldering. Sleep had brought a manner of rest, but as she sat up, yesterday's events rushed through her mind in a single moment of pain and fear.

Pa. The Man of Sap. Jose Luis. The bird.

Panicked, she twisted around to make sure John's bird was still there and let out a sigh of relief. It was impossible to miss the bundle of crimson feathers against the brown-gray trunk. The bird must have already left and come back, because a fat white earthworm hung from its beak. With a snap, it swallowed its breakfast.

She rose to her feet, ready to repack the satchel. Dizziness descended on her. Unsteadily, she put a hand on the tree for balance. Her legs cramped, the muscles spasming after spending the night against the tree. Travel took strength and she hadn't eaten since yesterday morning. Moving carefully, she lowered herself back to a sitting position and waited until the earth steadied beneath her. Then, with effort, she ate some jerky and sipped some water from the canteen. The jerky was tasteless. Wiping her mouth with the back of her hand, she pushed herself up, ignoring the tremors that danced up and down her legs.

The bird took off from its branch, gliding forward. Catalina fell in step behind it. Every few moments, she scanned ahead, trying to make sure the way was safe. After all, she was following John's bird, and it was almost as strange and horrifying as the Man of Sap himself.

Unexpectedly, the bird came to a perch on a branch. Catalina slowed. The bird ruffled its wings and bobbed forward and back on its talons. She recognized the behavior and her breath, which was already reedy from moving briskly through the woods, became even thinner. The bird was preparing to attack. Her?

Then she heard them. Footsteps. Human footsteps. Moving quickly in her direction.

Her hand flew into her satchel and closed around Pa's hunting knife. She pulled it out, unsheathed it. Then she shucked the satchel and the bulky jacket and crouched low by a tree, knife held out in front of her.

From the left, someone burst through the woods. It was a young man. He was *tall*, probably three inches over six foot. Aside from his height, the only other things Catalina saw were the ax he held and the bird he had leashed with a fraying piece of thin rope. Just like hers, it was one of John's birds. Unlike hers, it was wounded. Its side was bound in cloth underneath its wing, and blood dripped from it in heavy drops.

The young man saw her by the tree. His body tensed and he raised the ax. She didn't wait. Last time she'd hesitated, the Man of Sap took her brother. Never again.

She pushed off the tree, letting her body weight and momentum carry her toward him. All she had to do was swipe with her knife. It cut through the side of his forearm, but he didn't drop the ax. He staggered back, alarmed.

"Hey! That hurt!"

Pivoting, she prepared to attack again. A sudden rush of activity broke out. Her bird dove from its perch on the tree. It let out another caw. Only this one was shrieking, harrowing, poignant. It flew into the wounded bird, batting at it. With almost graceful ease, it struck its victim from the sky and to the ground. It wasn't finished. Before anyone could intervene, it slashed the wounded bird's throat with its talons. Blood gushed from its neck and its wings trembled against the ground. Catalina's bird squawked victoriously over the felled bird and then took flight in another burst of wind.

This time it flew at the young man, pecking at his face and arms. He fell back, trying to protect himself from the bird's assault. He swung the ax blindly, but the bird avoided the blade. It flew up to the tree behind Catalina and landed far out of the young man's reach. Angrily, it shrieked at him.

With the attack over, the young man focused on Catalina. Her chin tilted as she stared up at him—way up. Pa and Jose Luis were so small that she wasn't used to feeling small herself, but she definitely did now. Her grip intensified on the knife.

"Who are you?" she demanded. "Where did you get that bird?"

"How about we both take a breath?" He eyed her knife. "I'm not going to hurt you. Though you certainly haven't extended the same courtesy."

He set the ax onto the ground with overexaggerated motions and nudged it over to her with his foot. She picked it up with her free hand. Even holding the knife and ax, she didn't feel safe. He was about her age, yet his forearms and biceps were sharply defined, chiseled from the sort labor full-grown men did.

He asked, "Mind if I check on Rodger?"

"Who's Rodger?"

A quick jerk of the head indicated his bird. Catalina nodded, her back still pressed against the tree, the knife and newly acquired ax lifted. He bent down, wobbling a bit. Despite his broad shoulders, poor health inked itself across him. Reddish purple marks stained his eyelids and even his lips, just a tad.

Gently, he touched Rodger's wing and shook his head.

"Well, he's gone." He spoke matter-of-factly but his face tightened, as though sad his companion had met such an end.

"Where did you get that bird?" she demanded again.

The young man didn't immediately respond to her questions. Gently, he untied the rope from around the unfortunate creature's neck. Pausing for a moment, he was motionless aside from his fingers. Those worried the already frayed rope. He said, "I'm hunting the Man of Sap."

"You are?" Surprise loosened Catalina's grip on the weapons.

"Question is, what are *you* doing out here?" She imagined what he must see: a dark-haired girl in a jorongo, holding a knife meant for a man's hand. There wasn't much to impress him, but an admiring look settled over his face. She scowled. He had no right to approve of her. "Given the bird, I imagine you might be hunting him too."

"He—he took my brother." The sentence slipped from her lips before she could stop it. Saying it made her relive it. Made her see Jose Luis slung over the Man of Sap's shoulder, as lifeless as Pa. She blustered on. "Who's the Man of Sap to you? Why are you after him?"

"Name's Paul." Even though he was bleeding from the bird scratches and the knife wound, he spoke as easily as if they were meeting in town. "You say he took your brother?"

"I did. He's only thirteen." She cut herself off, swallowed hard. "It's why I'm following one of John's birds."

Catalina looked up at her bird. Paul's gaze lingered on her for a moment longer and then he stared at it as well. It snarled back down at them. Rodger's blood stained its beak and streaked across its wings, dark crimson against the bright red feathers.

"Odd," Paul murmured, eyes narrowed. "Your bird is in the peak of health. Only way I was able to catch Rodger was because he was already wounded. I tried to nurse him back to health before we left, but he wouldn't let me. Just took off. And how did you know his name is John?"

"I think . . ." She hesitated and decided to answer with a partial truth. "I think the bird is letting me follow it."

Paul waited, as though knowing there was more to the story. He didn't press her, though, when she fell quiet.

"Well." He took a piece of cloth from his pack and wrapped it around the cut from her knife, struggling to do it with one hand. "I can't say it's been pleasant meeting you because it hasn't. I'll be on my way—I just need your bird."

"*What?*"

"Yours killed mine. Quid pro quo and all that."

Catalina raised both the knife and ax again, glad she hadn't set them down.

"You're not taking the bird."

"Listen. I was hired to track . . . John, you said his name was? And cut down any of his trees I come across. I'm a lumberjack. One of the best." A grin of pride flashed across his lips. "That's the job, and I'm going to do it. If I come across your brother, I'll make sure to send him home to you. But I can't be slowed down by another person. I work alone."

"Who said I wanted to work together?" The presumption made her blood boil. "Alone is fine for me."

Paul barely seemed to hear her. He contemplated, as though trying to figure out how to catch the bird. Catalina took a breath through her anger.

"Good luck trying to wrangle the bird without me," she said sharply. "He won't continue without my say." That was a reach. Only minutes ago, she'd been worried it was about to attack her and she certainly didn't trust it. Still, she lifted her head and raised her hand. Meeting its glassy eyes, she said, "Come."

The bird shuffled in place on the branch. Paul leaned back and crossed his arms. The grin returned to his mouth, making her more annoyed. She focused on the bird again.

"Come," she repeated, stronger and louder.

It fluttered off the branch and flew down to her, landing on her hand. It was heavy, much heavier than she'd anticipated. She struggled not to shudder. Next to her face, the bloodstained beak glimmered, its feathers slick and oily.

Turning to face Paul, she stood there, bird on arm, chin up. The fabric of her jorongo draped between her arm and side, making it seem as though she had a colorful wing.

"I see." Annoyance pressed Paul's mouth into a thin line but he dipped his head, as though conceding. "Well, how about we just head in the same direction but separately? You won't even notice I'm here."

"Won't even notice you're here?" she snapped. "You're as tall as a Maypole."

"True, I'm a little difficult to miss." Cockily, he angled his head upward, sending Catalina's blood to yet another higher temperature. "But look. Every moment we waste, John has more time to scheme. How about we get going?" It was true. Time passing meant more time that Jose Luis was in John's grip. And, even if they hadn't gotten off to the best start, the lumberjack was hired to find the Man of Sap. He could have more information, information that could help her. "Besides . . . you might need someone strong like me, especially if you're tangled up with that man."

At that, Catalina took a swift step forward so she was under his nose. She raised her head to stare him straight in the eyes. "You can tell yourself that if you want. But it's you who needs me and my bird. Don't forget that."

A light flared in his gaze and there was no denying the slight smirk that passed over his face. But though he tried to hide it, she swore there was something more in his eyes. Something akin to respect.

Silently, he held out the rope to her. She tossed it aside and the bird left her arm to settle on a nearby branch.

"We won't need a leash."

"You certain?"

"Yes."

He nodded and waited as she slipped back into Pa's jacket, returned her knife to the satchel, and slung it over her shoulder. Abruptly, she handed the ax back to Paul.

"No firearm?" she asked, eyeing the empty belt that cinched his waist. Everyone traveled with firearms and she would've too, if Pa's rifle hadn't been broken.

Holding the ax with one hand, Paul flipped it up into the air. It spun around twice, light dancing off the blade like far-flung stars, and he caught the handle easily.

"Don't need one."

Seemingly pleased with his display, he swung the ax back and forth, demonstrating more prowess. Catalina rolled her eyes.

"As long as you can do more than throw it around," she said. "I doubt a bear would be threatened by how high you can throw an ax."

"Good old Bertha has never let me down."

"First Rodger, now Bertha. You really like naming things."

"It could be worse. I could like stabbing strangers with knives instead." He·launched the ax into the air again and, as he caught it, had the audacity to wink at her. Oddly, she was nonplussed but God knew why. No one could call her a stranger to teasing. She did have a little brother, after all. However, Paul's teasing made her uncertain, like she was exploring new terrain without a compass.

"I don't know what you expected. You came crashing through the forest like a wild animal. Enough playing around. We need to go."

"Playing around?" Dramatically, Paul pulled the ax close. "Don't listen to her, Bertha. She's just jealous."

He did, however, sheath the ax. The bird winged ahead, and they fell into step next to each other. For better or for worse, Catalina had a new companion.

CHAPTER FIVE
JOHN

AFTER THE FIRST CROP FAILED, I MET HIM. The banker. When I walked into his office at the bank, his back was to me, arm extended as he reached for a landscape painting on the wall. He shook his head, took the painting down, shook his head again, put it back.

I cleared my throat. He turned, faced me. I was startled by how beautiful he was. Not handsome or attractive. Beautiful, in the way a black dahlia or a northern widow spider is. Though I wasn't certain why, I felt a rush of excruciating loneliness, the sort that had colored my life until I met Marguerite. I wished I could retrace my steps to the time when I first kissed her and roll up the path I'd been on since purchasing my orchard and set it aside like a worn-out rug. Only it was much too late for that.

"I didn't see you there. Sincere apologies." The banker gestured to the painting. "I would've picked something different for my bank."

"Isn't this your office?" I was glad to speak and distract myself from the peculiar onset of bleak emotion. "Am I in the right place?"

"Oh yes. Yes, of course. I don't get to pick the décor, though, so it never feels quite right." He smiled, his lips framing brilliantly white teeth. Aside from the two larger front teeth, the rest were the exact same height and shape, rows of repeating pearly perfection. Men of his age (thirty, perhaps?) usually had crowded teeth veined with yellow. "It's baking soda."

"What?"

"You know it as sodium bicarbonate. Give it a try." Another beguiling smile revealed them. "It'll polish yours right up."

I clamped my mouth shut as we both sat down—he in a large, upholstered chair on the far side of the desk and me in a straight-back wooden one facing him. He reached into his desk, and I stared as he pulled out a bright red apple and a knife.

"Anyway, Johnny, what can I do for you?"

Effortlessly, he began to peel the apple. The knife flayed the skin easily and it curled onto his desk in a red spiral. I stared at it, my mind racing. Had I told him my name? Also, no one except my father ever called me Johnny. Not even Marguerite. His eyes remained on me as he peeled the apple, as though they were the blade cutting beneath my flesh to my most secret sins.

"My apple harvest failed." I tried to speak without showing my teeth or without staring at the apple. "Canker."

"Well, this is insensitive of me." The banker tucked the apple back into the desk, out of sight. "I'm sorry to hear that. It does happen. No shame in it, that's for certain."

No shame in it. The banker repeated the words Marguerite had said to me a few days ago. I knew they were meant to comfort, to soothe, and that she was trying to be helpful. But they did the opposite. They irritated, inflamed. She saw that they did. In fact, later that very day, I heard her praying over the Bible that had belonged to her father, murmuring about my look of sin. I'd hardly recognized her.

"I was able to salvage the trees. Cut out the canker. They'll produce next harvest."

"You sure about that? Sometimes the disease is deeper than it appears. Maybe you should cut them out by their roots. Plant new trees."

Cut them out by their roots. My beautiful trees. The thought nauseated me. Even if I could bring myself to destroy them, it would take eight years to grow new trees from seeds. There was no way I could wait that long. No way we could survive. I had to make these trees produce so we could make a profit next year. That was the end of it.

"I'm here to mortgage our house. I'll pay back the debt next fall. Can you help?"

The banker steepled his fingers and brought them to his lips. There was a moment of silence and it seemed as though he was posturing. Putting his fingers to the center of his lips to enhance the composition of his face. I couldn't imagine it was to impress me, so I assumed it was to amuse himself.

"I can help you." Once more, his smile returned. Somehow, though, it seemed narrower, sharper. "Let's make a deal."

❀

My trees recovered from the canker. Scars from where I dug out their lesions were visible, but they were healed over, new bark growing over the old.

"It worked," I triumphantly told Marguerite. "This fall, there will be apples and you shall have the very first one."

We danced in the kitchen, just as we had at the corn husking, and I saw the old sunshine in her again, beaming through the new clouds of worry and grief. I picked up Gabriel and nuzzled against his soft, squishy baby ear and whispered, "Papa is going to give you the biggest red apple you've ever seen. Not only will he give it to you, but he'll show you the star inside. Every year, we'll pick a special apple together and open it. Papa will always be there, no matter what."

Gabriel babbled and laughed and made the day even more memorable by taking his first toddling steps while we sat beneath York, one of the trees.

Everything seemed well and sweet again, as though our lives were spun from sugar. Then, one morning a few months later, I looked out my kitchen window and dropped my coffee. I ran out to my orchard, suspenders flapping and shirttail flying behind me. The first tree, Methuselah, was *moving*. Its bark rippled like the surface of a pond disturbed by a large fish beneath it. I came closer and recoiled. Thousands of bugs swarmed over Methuselah. I slapped and beat at the trunk, trying to shake them free but the tiny beasts started crawling up the sides of my pants.

I raced to the farmhouse and burst into the kitchen. Marguerite sat at the table, the now two-year-old Gabriel with her. At the sight of me, her face paled.

"The pestilence of Egypt," she cried. "Père used to preach about it. It's God's judgment."

Infuriated, I stomped over to the table and cleared it with a swoop of my arm. Plates and cutlery crashed to the floor in a crescendo of pewter and glass. I grabbed my agriculture books and dumped them onto the table. There had to be a way to stop this attack.

I didn't notice Marguerite fleeing the room with Gabriel until the bedroom door slammed upstairs. Compunction stung me, as painful as the swarm's bites.

Head hanging, I slunk upstairs, a few bugs trailing along behind me. I quietly opened the bedroom door. Marguerite knelt by the bed, Bible open atop the quilt, Gabriel at her side. She was praying in French, her hands not folded as one might think, but grasping the quilt. Her fingers clawed the fabric, her hands bloodless and purply white. Muttered prayers fell from her lips.

The sight frightened me. I'd never seen her like this. I almost left. But I made myself go to her and put my hand on her shoulder. Startled, she pulled back from my touch.

"I'm sorry." The phrase was old and tired on my lips. It seemed like I was always saying it, a reflex to appease her and mitigate her misery. "I'll figure out how to make it right."

She lifted her face. New lines of worry cut across her forehead, surprising me. I'd been so consumed with the orchard that I hadn't really looked at her in some time.

"I'm sorry." This time I meant it. I'd let the orchard come between us and I never intended for that to happen. Slowly, she put her hand over mine. I knelt behind her and wrapped my other arm around the soft hills of her shoulders. Her head found its way to the hollow of my neck. She fit so well there. She always had. Then she withdrew.

"You've lost yourself, John," she said, dully staring straight ahead. "Your obsession is fitting you for Hell. The Devil knows you're here and he wants your soul."

She bent back down over the Bible and resumed her muttering. I stood abruptly, feeling as though she'd stabbed me. Didn't she know I'd been born the son of a drunken devil but that I was different from him? That I'd worked so hard to be something for her? On the far side of the bed, Gabriel stared at us, eyes as big as quarter dollars.

Backing out, I shut the door and went back down the stairs with heavy steps. The prayers came with me. Followed me. Taunted me. Even though the kitchen was filled with the bugs and their rattling, they couldn't drown out the sounds of my wife's prayers. I heard them over and over, so much I couldn't think, couldn't hardly even seem to breathe. I clamped my hands over my ears, tilted my head back, and screamed wordlessly at the ceiling.

Lord knows what strange sounds rose to Heaven that day from our farmhouse. The jawing of the bugs, Marguerite's mutterings, and the cry from my own lips. Pure madness, I'm sure it sounded like. And pure madness it was.

CATALINA

Catalina's unease grew as she and Paul walked for nearly a mile in silence. She wished he wasn't here. Waves of grief over Pa's death alternated with desperation over Jose Luis's abduction. Feeling them there, next to a stranger, was almost more than she could bear.

Paul was the first to break the silence.

"We've established some names but what's this one called?"

"What?" Catalina stared blankly at him; her mind lost to tumult.

"The bird. Did you name it?"

"Oh." She pulled herself to the present to think of an answer and said cagily, "No. I haven't named anything since I played with dolls."

Paul lifted his hands in mock surrender, still peering at the bird that flew above them like a sentient kite. Catalina took advantage of his distraction to look at him. Really look at him.

His clothing was travelworn: faded plaid flannel shirt, sleeves rolled to the elbows, and trousers, torn through in both knees. Scruffy brown hair, though it needed a trim, waved pleasingly across his forehead. His face was, well, handsome. Very handsome, she realized with strange alarm. She glanced away in annoyance and then dared to look at him again. Despite the playful words that fell easily from his lips, she noticed the tense set of his mouth and the red, sleepless look in his eyes.

"You name it," she said impulsively. "I wouldn't want to deprive you of the pleasure."

"I don't think it wants me to."

Catalina hesitated. Naming a wild creature reminded her of Jose Luis and his winter mouse. What had he called the little thing? Don Pedro, after the Spanish pirate. It was an homage to their childhood. Don Pedro was often one of the many imaginary foes trying to breach their hideaway of branches and leaves. They always managed to stop him, though, vanquishing him with stick swords and magic spells.

"Well then . . . Don Pedro. The pirate."

At its name, the bird cawed, seemingly accepting his new rakish moniker.

"It's fitting," Paul said. "Our Don Pedro shall conquer the woods instead of the seas."

"Well . . ."

"What?"

"Don Pedro was caught."

"I see. A story with an ominous ending."

"A realistic ending," Catalina asserted. "He was hung with his crew."

"So, he died with his friends." The levity in Paul's voice dimmed, just a bit. Then he said, "Our bird has a name. What's yours?"

Catalina wavered. She needed to tell him, certainly, especially if they were traveling together. But somehow it seemed too intimate to tell him the name given to her by Mamá like a gift woven from love. Warily, she said,

"Catalina."

"Catalina." He spoke silk into her name, saying it with much grander inflections than she had. You'd think she was the lady of a large house and not an orphaned girl far from home.

"It's Spanish," she said quickly. "My mamá was from Mexico City."

"Mexico City? That's a ways away."

"It is." When Catalina was little, Mexico City felt close because Mamá talked about it all the time. As she grew older and

Pa uprooted them so much, she longed for it. Mexico City had represented home to Mamá, so it came to feel the same way to Catalina, even though she'd never been there. But she imagined the Plaza del Zócalo and how buildings with bell towers, terraces, and copulas rose to a bright blue sky, making you feel tiny. Mamá and her family had left during the War for Independence. She was Spanish and Indigenous, and therefore from a low casta. Her Padre betrothed her to a purely Spanish man to elevate her status and said the wedding would be held once they could safely return. But the war wasn't over before Mamá met Pa. So, while her parents eventually went back, Mamá moved to Pa's home in Wisconsin. Catalina never got to meet her grandparents. They were murdered by bandits preying on families traveling to get back to their homes. Mamá always described them as brave because they loved with open minds and open hearts.

"It's odd they managed to meet, him being from here and her being from there."

"Not odd. Romantic," Catalina interjected. It was the only story of Pa's that she still let herself dwell on, the one about how he'd worked for a trader. At that time, Americanos weren't allowed to trade in New Spain so if Mamá hadn't been displaced by the war, they wouldn't have met. Pa had spotted Mamá by a stall selling colorful skeins of yarn in an adobe town just outside New Spain. "My parents fell in love and got married in a tiny chapel on a property owned by a barón. There were so many candles lit that Pa was worried the chapel would burn down before the Rite of Marriage was finished. But Mamá wouldn't have had it any other way. She said the candles made the gold on the icons glow and it felt like she was in heaven."

Paul listened, an unexpectedly wistful expression settling over his face. It almost made her want to say more, to tell him about how her parents, on the first day they met, had walked along a creek. Mamá regaled him with stories about how the Plaza del Zócalo had once been the Aztec city of Tenochtitlan. Pa bought her a hot chocolate spiced with cinnamon and chili powder.

Catalina winced. Why was she sharing such personal details with Paul? Especially ones she held so close to her heart? Almost sternly, she said, "I've never been to Mexico City, or Mexico." Somehow, Paul had led her into her memories. Another one rose, Pa always saying "¡Ven aquí y bésame!" to Mamá—it meant, "Come here and kiss me." The thought was a string of fire that tugged Catalina's gaze to Paul. To his lips. Alarmed, she snapped her gaze away.

Paul didn't notice because he was too busy trying not to fall over. A low-hanging branch hung in their path, and he barely ducked in time. Clumsily, he righted himself. There was a quick tensing of his jaw. He was flustered, Catalina realized.

"Are you well?" she asked. "You seem poorly."

"I had cholera a few months ago," he said. "Just need clean air and sunshine. Soon, I'll be right as rain."

"Oh." Sickness was common. Dysentery, typhoid, scarlet fever, smallpox . . . there were hundreds of vile illnesses waiting to fill your lungs with phlegm and blood and kiss your forehead with fiery fevers. She pondered, trying to fill in the image of Paul. He continued.

"Could be worse. I reckon you've heard of the apple sickness?"

"No, I haven't. What is it?"

"Wild apple trees have been going rampant. And the apples are poisonous. They kill you."

"Kill you?"

"Kill you dead."

Catalina remembered the three apples sitting on their doorstep. The Man of Sap must have put them there, poison masquerading as sustenance. The water Pa had drank smelled of apples too—John must have put drops of cider in it. Three poisoned apples. One for each of them. He'd wanted to kill them all.

Paul continued, oblivious to her whirling realization. "It's why I'm out here. Little town about two days' travel from here lost some children after they ate the apples. Caused a huge row so they posted an ad for a lumberjack to go chop down the trees and, well, kill the Man of Sap."

Swallowing hard, Catalina tried to clear her mind.

"So . . . so you answered the advert?"

"I did indeed. Rodger had been wounded and captured by the townspeople. Once he was well enough, I put him on a rope, hoping he'd lead the way back to John. I figured he was my best bet at finding and killing the bastard. Pay is double if I do, so I'm motivated, to say the least. I'll be rich as a king once this is over."

"You're doing it for the money."

"Yep."

The answer was flicked toward Catalina without thought. It clearly didn't mean much to him, but it rubbed against her with the discomfort of an ill-fitting shoe. She didn't think there was enough money in the world to draw her after John.

"Do you know what you're up against?" she asked. "I saw him. He isn't human—he's—" Abruptly she stopped, thoughts disorganized and tattered.

"I'm not worried."

Worried. Catalina wasn't worried. She was scared. If Paul listened and knew what awaited them, he would be as well. His nonchalance was so palpable she could almost see it on him as though it were a jaunty cap he wore sideways.

"Well," she said, letting coldness settle into each syllable like frost. "You're lucky."

"Lucky?"

"You have only yourself to worry about and you can just . . . go home at any time and be fine."

The more she thought of it, the more annoyed she became. Lumberjacks had no end of work, so he had no urgent need for money. It must be the glory, then, the desire to slay a monster that sent him deep into these woods armed with nothing more than an ax.

Paul didn't respond, she realized, and she decided she didn't care. Still, she couldn't resist glancing quickly at him, a gaze so fast no one could pin it to her face if they tried. Somehow, the hollows under his red eyes seemed more prominent, the shadows thicker, like pooled, dark water.

No matter. She wouldn't let anyone distract her. Especially not the tall, mysterious stranger who walked beside her.

They walked in a cloud of tepid silence for the rest of the day, until the sun, fat and close, dropped itself into the trees. Bit by bit, darkness swooped in, as though the eye of the world had closed and trapped them behind its lid.

Paul said, "We should make camp."

"No." Panic, made toothier with urgency, sank into her. The day was over, which meant it was the end of the second day without her brother. "Let's keep going."

"I—I might need a rest." Paul's voice was so low it was almost buried beneath the skittering of the trees. "We've been going fast all day." She realized his breath came out in short pants, as though each one fought the other to get out and find air. "Besides, I'm not the only one. Look at Don Pedro."

It was true. Don Pedro glided close to the ground, wings angled back so he didn't have to flap them. Practicality won over panic.

"Fine then. But we begin again at daybreak."

They made camp quickly. Paul built a fire with practiced ease and soon they sat in the circle of its warmth. Even though the heat was hot on her face, Catalina held Pa's jacket tight around her. Plants drew their buds in like lips closing after drinking sunshine all day while squirrels, rabbits, and skunks folded themselves into their hovels.

While most of creation withdrew from the night, some stepped into it. Bats fluttered their leathery wings overhead and owls' eyes glowed green and gold from nearby branches. Snails glided down rocks and left their tracks behind. The tracks shone in the moonlight, making it seem as though the rocks wept thick, silvery tears. In contrast to the elegant snails, lumpy parades of hedgehogs waddled by.

Paul sat still but seemed to loathe it. His fingers jittered around his ax, and he shifted impatiently. The minute he seemed rested enough, he sprang to his feet. He swung his ax back and forth and tossed it into the air a few times. Catalina couldn't help but watch. She'd never been so entranced. The movements flowed into each other with a strange, fluid grace. The minute the ax returned to his grasp, it was sent spinning up again. The blade's edge reflected the fire, sometimes seeming to wink, sometimes seeming to grin. It cut lethally through the air yet Paul's hand was always there to snatch the handle before it fell too far. But then he missed one step and then another. His breath, which had settled, turned short again. Abruptly, he sheathed the ax and limped over to the fire, dropping down beside her.

Catalina stared hard into the flames. The despair she'd managed to ignore rose, as though it too was a creature that thrived on darkness.

With her whole heart, she wished she, Pa, and Jose Luis were back at their cabin. She never let herself picture what it might've been like if Mamá was alive, and now she had to apply the same rules to Pa. Thoughts—fantasies—they only held you back. Cut against reality, made you weak.

But sitting by this fire, far from the cabin and Jose Luis, she pictured it. Mamá, Pa, Jose Luis, and herself. It was like a poem. Not her poems, which were full of grief, but a happy one. Life with the ones she loved most. She pictured it for as long as she could, until the comfort slowly turned to a deep pain. It could never exist. Just like her poems couldn't either.

She didn't mean to, but she glanced at Paul, desperate to think of something else. He stared at the fire too. Somehow, he sensed her gaze and met it. She almost turned back to the fire, but something stopped her. They didn't say anything, and then she decided it made her feel worse that he was there, reading her grief in her face.

Well, he was right about one thing.

It was better to work alone. Having him here threw her off-balance. She rose to her feet, swiftly enough to startle him. He tilted his face up to look at her, but this time she refused to meet his eyes.

"I'm going to sleep."

Tensely, she walked to the other side of the fire, as though the distance would make him disappear. She took her blanket out of her satchel and draped it around herself. With Pa's jacket and Mamá's jorongo bundled tight against her, she lay down on the hard ground. Paul still sat by the fire, and she saw his silhouette shift as he looked over the flames at her. It was too dark to see his expression. She rolled onto her back.

Above her head glimmered a bafflement of stars. They scattered across the face of the sky like freckles, giving shape and light to its void. She closed her eyes, seeking the sort of nothingness that wipes away questions and hurts and grief. After a long while, it came.

CHAPTER SIX
JOHN

I TOLD MYSELF THE THIRD TIME WAS THE charm and it seemed like it was. The next year, my trees were heavy with promising buds that just needed to swell with life, and, when the time came, apples. Then, on a morning that seemed just like any other, I went outside and let out a cry.

My trees were covered in blights. I fell to my knees, covered in the cool of their shade, knowing that was all they would ever offer. Tears rolled silently down my cheeks. When I'd lost my first and second crops, I'd gathered my grief into energy, into purpose. This time was different. This time there was no manic swell of determination. The bank would take our farmhouse and my orchard. My trees, from Methuselah to Washington, would be ripped from the ground. Marguerite would leave me and take Gabriel.

It really was over.

I headed out for the bank the same morning, my thoughts consumed by my dying orchard and what it would do to Marguerite. Now, I think of that morning as the last one when my soul was mine, but perhaps it hadn't been mine for a long while. Perhaps I'd sold it to my desperate dream back when I bought my orchard against Marguerite's will and with her father's money. As it was, I planned to throw myself on the banker's mercy, beg him to extend my credit and forestall taking our land.

Instead, I found myself on a creaking stool, arms folded on a counter. As the bartender poured a shot of whiskey, I said—in a voice that sounded like my father's—"leave the bottle." The bartender arched an eyebrow but placed the bottle by my elbow. Swallow after swallow made the pain go away, replaced by a heady rush. What happened next is unclear. I see only fragments in my mind. My hand, the place where my wedding band used to be demarked by an absence of tan since I'd pawned it, throwing the door to our home open. The tilting hallway and stairs as I stumbled up them, their rippling making me feel as though I passed through mirages. For a fleeting second, my father standing in front of me, holding an apple. He'd been dead for five years.

Next, I was outside the bedroom door. In a way, it wasn't even my bedroom anymore. Lately, I'd fallen asleep at the kitchen table, poring over my notes. Only Marguerite and Gabriel slept there. I could hear her now, praying over that infernal Bible. The sound was like throwing a lit match on my whiskey-soaked mind.

In one violent motion, I kicked open the door. It burst open and Marguerite jumped to her feet, pulling our son with her.

"John? My God!" Her face went white, and she pushed Gabriel behind her.

"It's you," I slurred. "I know what you're doing! Those aren't prayers. You're putting a curse on me."

"What are you talking about?" she cried. I took a step forward and she cringed back against the bed. "Stay away from us!"

I lurched forward and they screamed. But I wasn't trying to get them. I snatched up her Bible and staggered back to the stairs. Leaning against the banister, I attempted to step down but lost my balance. Everything pinwheeled around me as I tumbled from the top to the bottom. With a crash, I landed in a heap in the kitchen.

An inane laugh burst from my throat and I almost thought it was from someone else. The Bible was on the floor right by me. I grabbed it as I got to my feet and fumbled my way over to the mantel. I snatched up the matches. Even though I was swaying on my feet, I managed to light one and hold it to the thin pages.

As I stood there, Marguerite and Gabriel came down the stairs, my wife clutching a carpetbag. Our eyes met as she paused in the doorway and her face somehow became even whiter as she saw the Bible burning in my hand.

The door slammed behind them and, suddenly, the boyhood loneliness that I thought I'd laid to rest long ago returned with a new, heartrending pain. It cut through the dizziness and rush of booze. The only two people I loved had fled, fled from me as though I was the Devil himself.

The Bible was engulfed in flames, and I threw it into the fireplace. Then I collapsed and everything went black.

I awakened to a thumping. At first, I thought it was just the pain in my head, pulsing away so hard I could hear it. Blearily, I lifted my head off the kitchen floor. The Bible was next to my face. White smoke wound from it in a thin, languid line, but other than that, it was intact. The thumping clarified into the sound of knuckles on wood. Someone knocked insistently at the door. With a moan, I pulled myself up. The kitchen shifted around me, and I swallowed hard, trying not to vomit. On wobbly legs, I made my way over to the door and opened it.

"Well, hello, Johnny." I lifted a hand to my eyes, shielding out the sun that backlit my visitor. What in God's name was the banker doing at my house? "Mind if I come in?"

He smiled his brilliant smile.

"Why are you here?" My mouth was as dry as sun-bleached bones. I stepped aside to allow him entrance. He let out a low whistle as he made his way to the kitchen.

"So here it is. Johnny Chapman's home. This is quite the setup. I can't say clutter has ever appealed to me, but I reckon a man can keep his place just as he wishes."

I looked at the room, seeing it anew. Half a dozen jars sat on the table, filled with water and soil for testing. Open books, stacks of paper, and tools scattered across the table and even the floor. To any normal eye, it was a frightful mess. A wave of embarrassment countered the haze of my hangover.

"Did you ever consider putting the table back against the far wall? It'd really open the space up. My bank—not the one you saw, my actual bank—well, it's a marvel of composition. Everything flows."

"Composition? Flows?" I put my hand to my head. I'd heard the words before but never in reference to the design of a room.

"I forget myself. I'm here on business. I'm sorry to say that the bank can't help you. You're up against it. It's sad, it truly is."

The banker gesticulated as he spoke and I watched his hands, fighting my rage, which seemed to grow with his every gesture. Here he was, in his fancy suit, with his perfect teeth, lording over me in my own kitchen. My own. What a farce. It wasn't even mine anymore, wouldn't be once the bank took it. "But I can help you."

"Help me?" My head shot up.

"That's why I'm here in your . . . lovely home. Now, I'll be honest with you, Johnny. You don't have anything to offer in the temporal sense, seeing as how the land and house belongs to the bank. There is something that you still possess, however. And it can get you everything."

"Everything?" The pounding in my head wasn't strong enough to drown out a sudden glimmer of hope.

"That's right. Everything. Question is, what is everything to you?"

I tilted my head to the side, tangled in his phrases and proclamations.

The banker seemed to sense my confusion and said, "What do you desire most? Do you want your family returned and restored to you?"

Marguerite. Gabriel. I closed my eyes, remembering how I wanted to give my son an apple from my orchard and dance with Marguerite through its trees. But then the sound of her prayers filled my mind. The tide of them washed over me and left me raw . . . It was fitting because Lord knew I'd only hurt her, despite my efforts not to. I could see their eyes, staring at me, confused, wounded, scared. Everything I did to wipe their hurt away only drove it deeper, every fix leading to another problem. I blamed Marguerite's change on her parents' deaths. But I'd been the one to force her into something she did not want and then kept her there, even as she dwindled more and more.

"I think . . ." I swallowed hard, forcing myself to speak the truth. "I think they are better off without me."

The banker nodded soberly.

"Sometimes that's the case with the ones we love." He appeared lost in melancholy thought for a moment. I wondered, suddenly, who his family was. Strangely, I couldn't imagine him with a spouse or children or even parents. He seemed a lone figure, not beginning or ending with anyone else, a creature forged at the exact age he was now.

The banker cast off his despondency and flashed his charming smile again. With the upturned crescent bright on his face, he said, "Well then, if that's the case, John, what do you want most?"

What *did* I want most?

The window to my right was large, framing the one thing I saw as true art. My orchard. At this distance, my trees looked strong and sturdy. Their branches stretched toward the sun from thick trunks. You'd never know disease ravaged them unless you were close. A potent wave of love came over me. Love for them, for what they were, for what they could be. I took a deep breath.

"I want my trees to grow."

The banker burst out laughing. The laughter had a harsh tenor and I imagined that if he snarled, it wouldn't sound much different. My face burned with shame.

"I'm sorry." He put a hand to his ribs. With effort, he composed himself. "The desires of men's hearts always, well, they confound me. Excuse me. That was rude." He steepled his fingers and brought them to his mouth, just as he had back at the bank. For a long moment, he considered me, and I felt trapped in his gaze, a veritable fly in the web of a sinister spider. "How about this, John. How about the gift of fecundity?"

"What?"

"Everything you plant will grow. Thrive. Gone will be your worries about canker, pestilence, and lesions." I narrowed my eyes. Perhaps he'd been nipping at the bottle, same as me. No man, no matter how rich, had that in his power. "You doubt. Understandable. But, if I could grant it, would you give me your soul as the payment?"

"My soul." I should be the one laughing at him. A soul wasn't something a man could take from another. I knew that. They were real in the way kisses were real, an immaterial electricity drawing us beyond the tangible in the way Marguerite had drawn me beyond myself all those years ago. Yet there was neither mirth nor madness in his gaze. "Impossible."

"Is it?" The smile stretched further across his face, thinning the crescent.

"It is." I intended to sound insistent, but my voice cracked. Probably because my mind was cracking. Not in the way glass cracks before breaking, but in the way an egg cracks before opening, releasing new life. "What would that mean? Giving you my soul?"

"Terms. I'm a banker, after all. If you fulfill the terms, you will be free to roam this earth for as long as you like. If you don't, well, you're a good old Baptist, aren't you? It'd be hellfire and brimstone and all that unfriendly, retributive business. Alternatively, you can always come to my bank and officially terminate the contract. That's something I offer everyone in your position freely."

Swallowing hard, I looked at the floor, at Marguerite's Bible lying at my feet.

"You're fitting yourself for Hell," she told me so often. *"The Devil knows you're here and he wants your soul."*

Marguerite had known it before me. My old town had too. I knew it now. I was the son of a devil, fit for Hell. But maybe I could avoid it—all while getting exactly what I wanted.

"With this deal, I would be . . . immortal?"

"Indeed."

"What would I have to do for you?"

"Plant."

"And everything I plant will grow?"

"Not just grow." He held his hands in fists and then unfurled them so his fingers extended, making his palms look like trunks and his fingers branches. Wiggling his fingers back and forth, he said, "Thrive. Everything would thrive."

I thought back to Governor Hull. How I'd stood in front of him and his cronies as they'd laughed in my face, unwilling to give a nobody from the backwoods a chance.

"I want more. I want to change the way people see farming in this territory. The land offers so much but no one is brave enough to experiment. I want to provide apples not just for myself but for everyone."

"So, a manner of renown and respectability? Why not? A fellow's got to have his recognizance." The banker rubbed his hands together like a hungry man about to devour a meal. He extended a hand to me. "Fecundity and fame. Do we have a deal?"

I nodded, slowly at first, and then faster. Deep inside me, in the place where this thing called a soul might live, I believed he could give me what I wanted. With a deep breath, I took the hand he offered.

It was the first time I'd ever touched him. I almost flinched. His hand seemed to widen and swallow mine, so much so that I no longer saw my hand at all, only his. It was cold and bony. Fighting the unsettlement, I met his gaze.

"It's a deal . . . well, almost," he said.

From his jacket, he pulled out a stack of papers and a fancy fountain pen. The pages were blank but, right before my eyes, words germinated, grew, filled them in. My name unscrolled across the top in calligraphy, curlicues and flourishes sprouting from each letter like leaves from a springtime bough. Tiny letters in the same calligraphy stretched out below. At the bottom appeared a black line awaiting my signature.

"One contract for fecundity and fame. Sign here, Johnny."

The pen was cold, like his hand, but I took it and signed my name.

CATALINA

Catalina awoke. Mist seeped through her blanket. Birds stirred in the high branches of the trees and a group of wild turkeys noisily left their roosts, crashing inelegantly to the ground from their nighttime perches. It was early, very early. Slowly, she sat up, body aching.

Don Pedro was awake and rubbing his wings against the trunk of a tree. Paul was still asleep, but his body twitched. Even though she was sore from the night on the ground, Catalina forced herself to her feet and stuffed her blanket, handful by handful, back into her satchel. They needed to head out. Joints stiff, she walked over to Paul. She bent to jostle him awake when he mumbled. It sounded like he said *no*.

It was hard to be certain, but she could've sworn that was what he said. Standing over him, she watched. It was odd to see him this way. Gone was the grimness he wore like a sober, gray coat. Instead, his head twisted from side to side and he looked . . . scared. And young, as though sleep took him back through the years. She should wake him. It's what she would do for Jose Luis if she heard him having a nightmare. But Paul wasn't anything like Jose Luis and she found herself frozen, hand stopped above his arm.

Without any warning, his eyes flew open, and he lurched upright. One hand shot out to grope for his ax, which lay at his side. Startled half out of her mind, Catalina jumped back, almost tripping into the smoldering remains of the fire.

"What?" Hazel eyes stared at her uncomprehendingly. "Where . . ."

"Are you all right?" She kept her distance. Blinking, Paul stared down at the ax he gripped. "I think you had a nightmare."

"I—" The lines of his face drew tight as he swallowed hard and slowly lowered the ax. "Yeah."

Catalina never dreamed. No images tormented her while she slept, or not any she remembered. But her sleep, when it came, was oppressive. Full of unnamed and unseen terrors that she never saw but sensed. Suppressing a shudder, she said, "Horrible things, aren't they?"

"Huh?" Sleepiness still clouded his eyes.

"Nightmares."

He set his ax down across his lap and rubbed his hands over his face. "I'll say."

A shiver ran through him, but he held stiff against it. Once it passed, he pushed his blanket aside and stood, as though he could push the nightmare aside as well. With purpose, he reached for his pack and pulled out a dented coffeepot, a small bag of cornmeal, and a jar of honey.

"What're you doing?"

"What does it look like? Breakfast."

"Breakfast?" Any sympathy Catalina had for him evaporated into incredulity. "No. We don't have time."

"We'll go faster on full stomachs." A small sack of coffee appeared from the same bag, followed by a tin mug. "You can't help your brother if you don't have the strength to get to him."

Everything in Catalina wanted to protest but she knew he was right. In fact, she hadn't even eaten last night. Couldn't.

"Fine. *Hurry.*"

She glanced at Don Pedro. The bird was enjoying a dust bath and didn't seem in any rush to leave either. She went to her satchel and took out some more jerky, grimacing as she realized she didn't have much left. Somehow, while following Don Pedro, she would have to forage and hunt. And maybe bathe, should they come across a river. Two-day-old sweat coated her skin. She ran her fingers through her hair, startled at how stringy it was—and even more startled when she glanced across at Paul, wondering if he noticed. Immediately, she put her hand down. Her appearance was the last thing that mattered.

Paul got the fire blazing again and though she didn't say it, the warmth was nice. The coffeepot went over the coals and he mixed cornmeal, water, and honey. Soon, the aroma of bubbling coffee and cooking combined with the fresh morning air of the new day. It was odd. Her stomach was nothing but knots of dread. Their camp smelled like breakfast, and breakfast belonged to a life where people awoke and ate before heading out to work in the fields and returned at the end of the day to join hands over a table. Not her life, where she followed a bird to rescue her kidnapped brother.

Still, it was oddly comforting. It was the sort of breakfast Jose Luis would devour. And she would too if she had some.

With meticulous attention, Paul flipped two hot hoecakes onto a tin plate. Then, he poured coffee into the mug. Steam rose from both. Holding the plate in one hand and the mug in the other, he walked over to her and sat down, close enough to brush elbows.

"I only have one set of dishes, so we can share."

For a moment, she didn't understand. Then she said, "But it's yours."

"Consider it payment for Don Pedro's services." He blew gently on the coffee and extended it to her, handle out. "Here."

"I . . . thank you." Taking the mug, she stared down at it, suddenly awkward. "I have jerky, if you want some."

"We can have it later," he said easily.

"Thank you," she said again, earnestly this time. Paul had a mouth full of hoecake and he waved a hand. She took one quick sip and then another longer one. Coffee was a luxury. It'd been years since she'd had some. God knew it was weak and the grounds were stale, but it didn't matter. It warmed her inside and out.

He traded her the coffee for the plate of hoecakes, and she broke off a piece with the fork and put it into her mouth.

"Is it good?" he asked.

She swallowed a mouthful of the warm and mealy cake. "What?"

"I didn't have much to work with, but I hope it isn't the worst breakfast you've ever had."

"Oh! You mean the food." Deadpan, she said, "It's terrible."

"Nooooooo." With a dramatic flourish, he threw a hand over his face. "Tomorrow, I promise a feast served on silver."

"It's the least you can do."

"Hey, I offered you three courses this morning. Coffee and hoecakes."

"That's only two."

"Third is my company." A smile dashed across his lips, and she almost smiled back into the broad warmth of his face. Then she looked down at the plate, echoes of last night's unease still reaching her. There was no reason for it, but he made something in her slip, just a little. Soften, like a piece of leather held so often it remembered the touch and became supple. She pushed the realization away. It wasn't true.

With a sharp breath, she extended the plate to him, as though she could hand off the strange, new feeling inside her. He gave her the coffee mug in exchange.

Quiet settled over them. Paul rotated the plate in his hands. Her hair, still undone from the night, curtained Catalina from him, but she could see his hands, circling the plate round and round. Irrationally, she wondered what it would feel like to have his hands circling her waist and spinning her into him. Her grip on the coffee mug tightened enough to imbalance it and send some of the precious liquid sloshing over the rim. It wept down her fingers in hot, brown tears. Quickly, she tried to hide her discombobulation by taking a long sip. Bitterness swept across her tongue and down her throat, and she let it sweep away the ridiculous idea of dancing with him too.

"So," Paul said, and she jumped at his voice. "Easy, gunslinger. You all right there?"

"Of course I am. You're the one having nightmares, not me." No one could accuse her of being soft now. She stared into his startled eyes unrepentantly. Methodically, he set the plate down. When he looked up, dark light glittered far within his gaze. She waited, expecting him to be angry, wanting him to be angry. If he was, then she could be angry back and this nonsense of softness could die a quick death.

He said blandly, "I was only going to ask what John wants with you. Or your family."

Catalina pinned her gaze to the mug's rim. Matching his tone, she said, "I don't know."

"Fine," he muttered.

"My pa told us stories about John." The sentence burst from her mouth as though it longed to find its way to him despite her. "But he should have simply told us the truth."

The empty annoyance at Paul shifted shape and became confusion and grief. Pa had lived life as though they and their series of poorly constructed cabins were beneath a fancy glass cloche with a blue sky painted on the underside of the dome and dried flowers held in place with pins. He whistled, sang, told stories. But just as often, Catalina would find him staring into the woods, eyes shiny with a curious gloss. For all his whimsy, it seemed like his heart was one of paraphernalia in the cloche, stuck through with a pin and displayed for her to see.

Yet for as much as she resented him, she'd never considered that maybe there'd been a reason he stared into the woods.

"I—" Discreetly, she slipped one hand into her pocket. She'd since shaken out the glass, but the rims of his glasses still lay there, twisted. "He died two days ago."

"Two days ago?" Paul's head shot up. "I'm sorry."

Determinedly, she kept going, anxious to brush aside his sympathy and the raw loss filling her heart and threatening to spill through her. "I think I misunderstood him."

"Your pa?"

"He was . . . gentle. And I had no patience for it. Most of the time I was frustrated with him." She was losing against the grief. She felt like she could taste it on her tongue, as metallic as blood, as bitter as alkaline. The only thing she could do was try to change the subject. "Anyway. It's no matter."

"It kind of is. He just passed, Catalina." Concerned kindness filled Paul's gaze and Catalina almost wished to let the pain river through her, to surrender to it in some way. But this was not the time and Paul was not the person to witness such a thing.

"Jose Luis will take it hard," she said. Silence fell and she was glad for it. Clearing her throat, she finally asked, "Are you close to your pa?"

The silence lasted a second or two longer, as though Paul wasn't sure they should switch topics. Then he followed her lead, letting them leave the conversation about Pa's death behind.

"You mean, my *father*. He's a formal man. I'm surprised he didn't have me call him Sir. He's a schoolteacher out in Minnesota. Always wanted to teach at one of those fancy universities but he never got the chance. Made him bitter as all hell."

"A schoolteacher? Did you grow up around books?" It was impossible to keep the eagerness out of her voice.

"My father has a large library."

Catalina had never been to a library, but she imagined it. Rows of bookshelves. Leathery spines forming a burgundy, brown, and black rainbow. Titles etched in gold along their lengths, making you scrunch your neck and turn your head sideways so you could read them. She pictured Paul leaning against a bookshelf, his head bent over an open book, eyes wandering across the page like a traveler moving into a new world. The image was as poignant as poetry.

"Did it have poetry books?"

"It did. Milton, Spenser, Dante. Several others."

The names didn't mean anything to Catalina, but she imagined each belonged to a writer who heard the mad howl of their own soul and wished to find words to describe it, just as she used to. She pictured the library once again, only this time she was there with Paul, reading Dante—whoever this Dante was—and exploring whatever realities lived in his books.

"The bastard was prouder of his library than anything else." Paul cut into her fantasy. "He would spend hours in that stuffy room."

Instantly, the picture of the two of them in the library evaporated. "So, you don't like reading?"

"Who wants to read when you can find stories out here?" He gestured with the coffee mug to the surrounding wilderness. "You can't find anything equal to this in a *book*."

Book was spat like a curse. She didn't understand. Not only was he gallivanting about the woods on some mission for money, but he also disdained something she could only dream of: access to books. Not just one, but many. And some of it was poetry.

"Seems like you don't realize just how lucky you are," Catalina said peevishly. "I would love to own books."

"Ah, yes. There's that word again. *Lucky*."

"Well, you are."

"You don't know anything about it."

"I know you grew up with books. Seems like the definition of lucky."

"Sure." He motioned to their shared plate. "Done?"

A sharp retort rose on her tongue, but she swallowed it back and nodded. They both stood, brushing hoecake crumbs off their clothing. They didn't say anything as they rinsed off the cutlery and packed up their small camp.

At least Don Pedro was oblivious to the tension. He stretched his wings, and suddenly, he froze. Then he lurched ahead, letting out a sharp caw.

Catalina exclaimed, "What in the . . ."

A shivering shook through the trees. Something sped through them, low and swift. Don Pedro arched his head back and cawed again. This time, there was a response. Caw after caw.

"John's birds!" Catalina cried as a red tide tore through the trees. At least twenty blurs of sharp talons and crimson feathers raced toward them.

There was only one thing to do.

Run.

CHAPTER SEVEN
JOHN

THEN AND THERE, I KNEW SOULS WERE real. Knew because I felt mine as it left my body. It didn't want to go. It writhed and fought and burned like hellfire all the way up from my chest. Nothing could stop it, but it tried to stay, tried to claw and scrape its way back. Whatever summoned it forth was too strong. It scorched through my throat, and out of my mouth. There was nothing to see. No floating light or glow. But I *felt* it, the part of me that held the ineffable human spark being cruelly ripped from me.

Suddenly, a rope looped around my neck. I fell to my knees as it choked me and grappled to get it off. Vaguely, I realized it wasn't a rope, rather a thick strap.

"Calm down, Johnny." The banker's voice was garbled in my ears, which popped as though full of water. He yanked me upright. I flailed in his arms. The strap at my throat released. Moved down and stopped just at my shoulder, as though finding the place it sought.

A burlap sack hung from the strap. It was so heavy that I was yanked violently to one side. With a cry, I tried to sling it off. But no matter what I did, it swung between my arm and hip. It felt as though my skin was only nerves, as though there was nothing beyond the scratchy fabric, the gouging strap, the heavy bag.

"It's what you wanted." The banker spoke evenly. "Every seed you plant from the bag will grow into an apple tree. It's in the terms."

Horrified, I grabbed the strap with both hands and jerked. I only succeeded in making the strap bite further into my shoulder.

"What terms?" I choked out.

"What do you think the contract stated? Plant the seeds in the bag. Should you ever get to the bottom, you'll be released from the task."

I yanked open the mouth of the bag. Apple seeds filled it to the top, each one a perfect black teardrop. They shook, the whole shining, antlike lot of them, alive and eager, longing for my touch. I plunged my arm into the bag. The silky seeds swallowed my arm whole as I tried to find the bottom. My hand strained, my delicate finger bones overextending and stretching in their joints. But there was no bottom. Only more seeds. I yanked my arm out and turned the sack upside down. Apple seeds gushed out in a gleaming, cascading wave. They pooled onto the floor and around my ankles. No matter how much I shook the bag, they kept coming.

Then my eyes began to fill with a sticky substance. It welled fat and heavy in my lids and clung to my lashes. The backs of my hands hardened, soft skin solidifying into . . . *wood*?

"It'll take some getting used to." The banker reached over to pat my shoulder. "But I gave you a little something extra, just for you. White teeth."

I clawed at my eyes, at my skin, at the bag, at myself.

"I want to go to your bank! I want to terminate my contract."

"You are more than welcome to visit, and if you do, I'll happily release you. But I'll be honest. No one has ever found it."

"No! I don't want this." My fingernails dug through the bark on my skin, peeling it away to find more underneath. "Please, please, I beg you, undo this."

There was no response. I turned in a circle, the bag throwing me off-balance. The banker was gone. I sank down to the floor. Half buried underneath the seeds was Marguerite's Bible. With trembling hands sprouting leaves, I picked it up.

Everything was gone. My family. My dream of growing apples from my orchard to proudly give to everyone. My soul.

I brought Marguerite's Bible to my face and cried tears of sap.

I didn't learn the true nature of my curse until later. At first, I thought it was simply these two things: my body was transformed, and I must plant the seeds.

And plant them I did. If I didn't—if I don't—well, you've seen. But I don't think you can fully understand how heavy the sack grows. How it becomes a knife-edge against my shoulder, digging in until the sap that has replaced my blood streams down my arm and drips off my fingers.

It's all I can feel.

All I can think about.

It's slow, incessant torture that builds in the same measure with each passing minute until I'm nothing more than an instrument singing a single note of agony and I must stop it.

Now when it happens, creeping blackness overcomes me. In the early years, it wasn't that way. But I'm getting ahead of myself. That change is its own dark chapter in my story, one I must fortify myself to tell.

At first, I sank into the depths of self-pity. The first few months, I searched fruitlessly for the banker's bank. It was a fool's errand and I soon realized it was as mercurial and sly as he, unfindable. Yet after the first year or so (how it blurs together!), I found pleasure in my new life. The miles I trod between towns teemed with life. When there were dirt roads, starlike myrtle and sunburst dandelions formed a sky of their own across the ground, one where day and night met. Wild daisies grew in dense skirts around them, as though trying to attire them for a party.

My favorite, though, was to be in the bosom of the woods themselves, with my brethren: trees. They grew proudly toward the sky like so many thousand Towers of Babel. The oldest were so tall I wondered if their uppermost leaves didn't reach God himself.

The woods were a home for many. I passed the Iroquois of the East, the Chippewa and Potawatomi of the Midwest, the

Crow and Shoshone of the mountains and Pacific, watching as they tried to defend their homes against the invasion of the United States government. They were also thoroughfares. When I traveled closer to the South, I saw silent groups of Black freedom seekers escaping the cruel bonds of slavery. They traveled at night and slept during the day, always listening for the baying of blood-hounds. Nature helped them. The North Star was a fixed point of promise in the sky, and it guided them. The trees also helped. Moss grows on the north side of the trunks because it seeks humidity and thrives in darkness. When it was too stormy or cloudy to see the North Star, they felt for the moss. When I made my way out to the wider plains, I encountered antlike strings of covered wagons heading west. As the years went on, those plains became dotted with abandoned furniture. Pianos, dressers, dolls, clothes. There were graves too. Makeshift and lonely, marked by two sticks tied together. Sometimes, when I headed southeast, I found swampy bogs and marshes. Every place, it seemed, had people, for those too had shacks, shanties, and docks slumping over green water.

Through my travels, I found apple trees in unexpected company. The Cherokee in the Southern Appalachians had long been cultivating apples. I didn't reveal myself to them, but I watched, feeling kinship with how they tended their trees. In Virginia, I learned enslaved people were forced to plant, tend, and harvest apple trees for Thomas Jefferson on his Monticello Plantation. The Cherokee and the enslaved people had already achieved such advancements in apple agriculture, I had a million questions I wished to ask them, if only I could show myself.

Every time I slipped seed into open fields near towns, I was elated. The seeds would bring the life I could never bring to my own orchard. Once my seeds grew into mature trees, there would be apples for everyone. Of course, no one knew it then. It takes several years for seeds to grow into producing trees. I could hardly wait.

Beyond that, my mind seemed to be a tree itself and I understood them in a way I never had before. Every day was a discovery. I'd always loved apple trees but now I marveled, awed by the intricate systems of life contained within them, how they were like little universes or oceans or civilizations, so infinite yet so sufficient.

I poured this information into long missives and sent them to the Michigan Territory government and then the newly formed Wisconsin Territory Horticultural Society, simply signing them "John." The men who once dismissed me now clamored for my letters. They sent a representative to lecture at universities on my behalf, and eventually the representative was even invited to the White House, where he shared my findings in Congress and had an audience with President John Q. Adams. Through my letters, I helped lay plans for state-funded commercial orchards, the very concept I'd been mocked for.

No matter how miserable the seed sack made me, I knew I was shaping the agricultural future of not only the Wisconsin Territory, but of the United States of America and Canada.

I imagined Gabriel eating one of my apples. He wouldn't know it was from me, but it didn't matter. Even though he could never know what I'd become, I would nourish and provide for him in the ways I'd failed before. Maybe Marguerite would eat one too.

Oh, if that were only the case. But it wasn't. A hellish reality awaited me, one that wouldn't reveal itself for ten years.

CATALINA

Overhead, the birds cut through the air, angling lower and lower. Paul yelled something but he was drowned out by the cawing. Together, they ran for all they were worth.

Branches slapped her in the face. Stirred up by the birds, a colony of cottontails dashed by in a zigzag pattern at her feet, ears flat against their heads. Field mice, squirrels, and quails scattered, disappearing into the overgrowth and up the trees.

But the birds weren't after the woodland animals. They were after *her.*

She had to escape. If she didn't escape, Jose Luis wouldn't escape. Her life was linked to her brother's, always, and now she ran for them both.

Ahead of her, Paul suddenly staggered and fell. Catalina raced to his side.

"Get up!"

Shadows fell over her face. Above her, the birds arched upward. There was only time to pull the hem of Pa's jacket over her head for protection.

The birds descended. Sharp talons dragged across her face and shoulders. They didn't reach through Pa's thick jacket or the jorongo, but they sliced across her forehead. One of Paul's hands was near her foot, fingers splayed and anchored against the ground. It was all she could see of him. The birds converged on him, a writhing mass of razor beaks and flailing crimson wings. She grabbed the hand. Pulled. He managed to stagger to his feet, face grim with desperation. One hand pressed to his chest.

"Come on!" Catalina dragged him forward and they broke into a run again.

With discordant shrieks, the birds streamed after them, weaving around the trees. Catalina knew that, even as fast as they fled, they weren't going fast enough. The birds would catch them again, shred them to ribbons.

Then, a dilapidated shack with boarded up windows appeared ahead. They raced to it and up the creaking, sagging steps. Paul turned his shoulder and rammed it against the door. It broke open. They plunged through it, practically falling across the threshold. Don Pedro slipped in with them. Just in time, they slammed the door shut and pressed their weight against it. It rattled and shook as the birds threw their bodies against it.

Strange sounds rang out. Sharp caws of pain followed by harrowing, agonized chirps. The onslaught against the door stopped and, eventually, quiet fell.

"They must have left," Catalina gasped. "It's over."

She noticed Don Pedro. He perched in the rafters of the cabin, anxiously bobbing up and down. Had he been fleeing from the other birds as well?

Suddenly, Paul's knees folded, and he sank to the floor. His shoulders pressed heavily against the door and his chest rose and fell fast.

"Are you all right?" Catalina asked. Dark purple flushed across his face like a bruise spreading across skin. A slight nod of his chin was his only response. She waited, unsure what she should do. After a bit, his normal coloring rose through the purply hue, and his breathing fell back into a rhythmic pattern. The cholera had turned him inside out, it seemed. His bleary gaze fixed on her forehead.

"You're bleeding."

Catalina wiped away a thick trickle of blood threading its way down her brow. Hesitantly, she said, "So are you."

He'd withstood the worst of the birds' attack. The shoulders and back of his shirt hung in shreds off his shoulders. Fresh cuts sent trails of blood down his chest.

"It's just scratches." An attempt to shrug made him wince and he tried to cover the wince with another shrug. "My shirt is done in, though." He reached for his pack and pulled out another one.

"Here. Let me help." Catalina stooped over him. Her legs trembled and she wiped her forehead again. Sweat mixed into the cut, making it sting.

"I'm fine."

"Don't be stupid."

He fumbled with the buttons on his shirt, a crease appearing between his eyebrows. Under his breath, he muttered, "I'm not."

"What?"

"Stupid."

Granted, it wasn't the nicest thing to say, but the amount of hurt in his tone confused her. "I only meant that you need to think." The furrow between his eyebrows deepened even further and she didn't know if it was from concentrating on the buttons or if it was something else. "Stay still."

Catalina brushed his hands aside and opened the new shirt. She didn't mean to stop but did. Never had she been so near to someone . . . like him. Her eyes ran quickly across his torso. There was no reason for surprise. Already, she'd seen the rise and fall of muscles along his arms. It made sense the rest of him matched, but seeing the sharp plains of his stomach and chest made her uncertain. Her gaze latched onto a pink and white scar mottling its way across his side. She traced its path with her eyes, grateful for the distraction from how intriguing she found his form. Paul noticed.

"It's from a logging accident."

"Well, you might have some more scars from the birds." Using the torn shirt, she daubed at the cuts crisscrossing his shoulders and chest. "And your shoulder is bruised from breaking down the door."

He shrugged with the uninjured shoulder. "Pain doesn't bother me. Or, not this kind, anyway . . ."

She waited to see if he'd continue. He didn't.

When Paul's cuts had been tended, Catalina helped him into the new shirt, and he fished some extra cloth out of his satchel. Facing her, he lifted it as though to press it to her forehead. At the last moment, he stopped and, with a sharp breath, handed it to her instead.

"For your face."

She took the cloth and wiped away the blood. A shudder forced its way over her body, an aftershock from the attack. Self-consciously, she glanced at Paul. He didn't say anything, but he nodded, just a bit. It was unclear what the nod meant. Maybe he was saying it would be all right or maybe he was trying to impart bravery to her. Regardless, it did make her feel better.

The quiet outside lasted long enough to make it seem safe. They stood and Paul unlatched the door. Catalina's eyes widened as they stepped out of the cabin. There were deep scratches on the door, but the most shocking discovery was scattered across the ground. The birds were entangled in a final scene of carnage. Talons tore into each other's necks, revealing thin ropes of the trachea, esophagus, and spinal cord. Beaks gouged through each other's bodies and their feathers were drenched with organ matter and blood. More blood pooled around their forms in lurid puddles, and their eyes stared sightlessly ahead.

Don Pedro shrank back from them, head ducking in fear.

"I think they turned on themselves," Catalina gasped. "Tried to eat each other."

They made their way down the rickety steps, and she knelt near the closest bird. Don Pedro landed next to her and huddled close. He let out a sound that was much more chirp than caw. For once, he seemed frightened. Catalina looked from Don Pedro to the dead bird.

"They're different," she murmured.

"You're right." Paul let out a low whistle. "These birds make Don Pedro look as ordinary as a loaf of bread."

It was true. Don Pedro had his bladed back and wings tipped with porcupine-like needles. The dead bird was also red and about the same size, but it had cloudy, milk-white eyes with a tiny dot of red for the pupil. Its feathers deteriorated into raggedy clumps, as though a mouse had gnawed them to bits. Tiny, baby-sized teeth lined the outside of its beak in rows. Catalina shivered.

"These aren't the birds that follow John," she said. "But then . . . where did they come from? And why would they come after us and then turn on each other?"

Were there more powers at play than just John? Her heart, which had finally calmed, began to pound. She'd thought the Man of Sap was her only enemy, yet these didn't seem to be his birds. Even more unnerving was the realization that Don Pedro, John's agent, was as frightened as she.

Unnerved, Catalina touched her finger to the dead bird's beak. Even though her touch was light, the small teeth were so sharp they broke through her skin. Two droplets of bright red blood welled on her fingertip. She stood.

"Do you need to sit? You're pale," Paul asked.

"I'm fine." With a brisk motion, she tossed her hair back, attempting to seem calm. The trees around them suddenly seemed like silent specters, warning of horrors yet to come. What else was hidden deep within these woods? No matter what prowled in the shadows, she would be brave. She had to be, for Jose Luis. But she also would be prepared. Sliding her hand into her satchel, she pulled out Pa's knife along with the rope. It only took a few moments to slip the rope through the loops on the sheath and tie it around her waist.

Now she could draw it quickly, should the need arise.

That evening at their camp, Paul drew his ax again. He sent it dancing through the air. Catalina watched, finding herself lulled.

Night threw its heavy mantle over them and soon Paul and his ax were just another shadow. He returned to the fire, and they settled in for bed. It happened again. Paul's nightmare. Catalina wrapped herself in her blanket and listened to the mutterings that streamed freely from his mouth. He said no, over and over, and then something about getting worse. Then it seemed as though the dream changed, and he was talking to his father.

In the morning, he moved like someone who'd had too much whiskey the night before, squinting, wincing, all the while trying not to. Silently, he made breakfast and Catalina sat on her blanket, pondering the mystery that was Paul.

"How long were you tracking John before we met?" she asked once they settled down to eat. Paul was staring at the ground and didn't seem to hear her. "Paul?"

"What?"

She repeated the question.

"Oh . . ." He frowned and handed her the mug. "About two weeks."

"That's a while."

"Yeah. Well. The bounty makes it worth it."

"The pay."

"Yep."

"Is there a reason why—why you have nightmares?"

The sizzling fire and sound of Don Pedro pecking at a line of ants on the ground was her only answer. She waited.

"Sort of." He spoke softly and she leaned closer to hear, but he was already pulling away. He picked up another stick and poked at the logs. The disturbance caused a shower of embers to swirl around them like angry orange fireflies. "It's my business."

There it was. The clear line that he would not let her cross, and she couldn't blame him because she had her own. All they could do was stare at each other from their own places of silence. But even as she understood, sparks of anger ignited in her chest, just as hot as the ones from the fire. Wasn't it her bird they were following? He was after John for nothing more than money—she was after John for the life of her brother. Testily, she said, "Your business has become mine."

"Not as far as I'm concerned. How would you like it if I asked about your dreams?"

"It wouldn't matter. I don't dream."

"Well." An empty smile twisted the corner of his mouth. "Sounds like you're the lucky one this time."

She took a sip of coffee but didn't taste it. An absence of dreams didn't mean an absence of nightmares. It only meant that hers were empty blackness, as big and crushing as a night sky with no stars to pin it up and keep it away. It was full of horrors that she didn't see, only felt, upon waking. It was contradictions; roaring silence, icy heat, eternal seconds.

Though she didn't want to admit it, she understood why Paul didn't want to talk about his nightmares. She didn't either.

As they followed Don Pedro, Catalina felt like she should apologize to Paul. The urge, though, enraged her. Why should she apologize? For prying about his nightmares? True, she had been rude to him. But she didn't understand him, and the lack of understanding felt threatening, like it might be her undoing. She focused on that thought and not the fact that, for the second day in a row, he'd made her breakfast.

A forbidden thought crossed her mind. Pa had been an enigmatic burden. Jose Luis was her responsibility. What would life be like with someone who was her equal? Someone who she could trust and rely on, who would protect her as much as she protected them? Such a life would have more room, wouldn't it? The answer came gently, as though whispered with love. Room for poetry and breakfast. *No.* There was no place for such thoughts, especially not now. Mercilessly, she buried the whisper.

CHAPTER EIGHT
JOHN

WHEN MY TREES WERE ABOUT TO MATURE and bear their first harvest, I sensed it, deep inside, and was thrilled. I could make the long trek back in time to see some of my trees in their full growth and maybe watch from afar as townspeople enjoyed their bounty. Sadly, I wouldn't be able to try them myself, as I got my nutrients from the sun, water, and soil and didn't eat human food any longer.

I headed back to where it all began: Wisconsin, near Eagle River. It wasn't hard to find one of the fields I'd sown.

I stared, awed. The plot had transformed from a weedy field to an enchanted orchard. Trees spread out in perfect rows. I walked among them, feasting my eyes on their beauty. I was fed, even though I couldn't eat their offerings.

The trees were an exquisite amber color and the branches extended from them in a scrolling filigree. Each branch was bejeweled with apples. They were a breed I had never seen or heard of before, despite my extensive travels. The apples were the darkest red possible and reflective, their surfaces doubling the images of everything around them. Rubies themselves could not be more breathtaking.

Father, they breathed, leaning toward me. *Welcome. We wish to show you how powerful and fearful we are. We wish to make you proud.*

"Oh, but you do. You make me so proud."

The praise rolled readily off my tongue and, deep inside me, there was a prick of compunction. Such things should be said to a child. Gabriel. Yet here I was, saying praises for him to my trees.

Watch, father.

On the far end of the orchard, a girl slipped in between the rows. She wore a high-necked blue dress. Her blond hair was neatly braided, plaited with ribbons, and coiled around her head.

Around me, the trees let out shivery sounds of anticipation. One of the branches lowered toward her and she reached for an apple. A smile broke across her face. I sighed, happy.

The girl took a bite, and her expression was bliss. She chewed slowly at first and then faster and faster, until her jaws moved with the speed of a grasshopper gnawing a fresh blade of grass. Golden juice dripped down her chin, hands, and off her elbows.

Then it happened. She bent double, clutching her stomach. Her face, which had been so joyous, twisted and contorted. She fell to her knees and rolled onto her back. The juice that stained her chin, hands, and arms bubbled on her skin and she screamed, clawing, trying to wipe it off.

Go to her, father. You must show yourself to her.

My trees whispered in my ears, and I went, shaking, afraid. I wanted to help but I didn't know what to do. Around me, birds with red feathers and sharp talons landed on the branches of my trees. They began to sing. Their song rang out, a mournful mix of high and low notes, all in a minor key. It was so beautiful and heartbreaking that tears ran down my barky cheek. Real tears, not the sap I'd grown accustomed to.

The girl saw me, and she whispered, "Mutter."

She was asking for her mother—I believed in German—and I watched as the light of life flickered and then left her eyes. As it did, the birds' chorus grew louder until it was more of a screech than a song, and a sudden wind whipped about the trees, as though the world itself was angry with me. Then it settled and everything fell silent.

I rose to my feet. I had no weapons. No ax or even a knife. It didn't stop me. With a cry of anguish, I grabbed a branch on one of the trees and ripped it off. I plucked the leaves from it and tore them to bits. But when I looked up, the branch had already regrown.

Your hands cannot hurt us, father, the trees whispered reproachfully. *We do your work. Do you not love us for it?*

I stared down at the body of the girl and the half-eaten apple at her side. Then I turned away and left.

CATALINA

They'd gone a few miles when Catalina noticed something strung between two trees. She asked, "Is that a clothesline?"

"Sure seems like it."

Cautiously, they investigated. It was indeed a clothesline. They stared, bewildered to find the domestic image out in the woods. Ivory silk tablecloths, each one featuring a wide border of embroidered lace, hung from the tightly clamped teeth of clothespins. The breeze exhaled through them, making them swing like restless, trapped ghosts. The line had been hanging there for a long time. The tablecloths bore evidence of both sun and rain, the fabric bleached away beneath streaking water stains.

"And look—just beyond." Catalina ducked beneath the tablecloths. "It's a town. Or used to be one."

A semicircle of buildings sprawled before them, a mismatched collection of frame shacks, cabins, farmhouses, and businesses with square fronts. Eerie sounds of abandonment wailed through the clearing: creaking doors, listing rocking chairs on porches, branches scraping in high-pitched discordance against windowpanes. Ivory ribbons, just as faded as the tablecloths, danced in the breeze from porch posts and doorknobs.

"What happened here?" Paul asked, hand on his ax. "What made everyone leave?"

"Children were here too. Look."

The green rectangle of a chalkboard loomed through the window of a clapboard building. Slowly, Catalina climbed the three steps leading to the door and pushed it open. Lines of desks, the chairs sitting in cast iron brackets and unfolding into small tabletops, faced the chalkboard. It brought back her own memories of school. That was before Pa had pulled them up at the roots, packed them into a rickety, rented wagon, and tipped them and all they possessed onto a small plot of land in the wilderness, a plot they would soon leave behind for another and then another. It came rushing back to her. The sound of chalk scratching across the board. The smell of almond-sweet paper. The sight of color-blocked maps and alphabet cards strung around the room like bunting.

Even more vivid was the memory of how she'd felt, just inside her chest—a glow, not the angry red sort of an ember being stoked into a fire, but the warm yellow sort that haloes a candle. There had been so many words to learn and once she did, she could weave them in her own ways, making a tapestry to lay over the world and see it anew.

The floorboards creaked underneath Catalina's steps, as though testy to be woken from their solitude. Someone had written on the chalkboard. The writing was an angry, garish scrawl. Drawing near, Catalina squinted at it. It seemed to be a schedule for a wedding day:

10am, bedroom with bridesmaids, get dressed.
12pm, ceremony, church.
2pm, dancing, barn.

The three sentences repeated over and over, horizontally and vertically. She turned around to ask Paul what he thought, but then stopped.

He was bending over one of the desks, hands anchored on either side of it, and for a moment she thought he was out of breath again. But that wasn't it. A book sat open on it, and he stared down. Even from her distance, she could see muscles tensing in his arms and bunching in his shoulders, tension coiling through him. Strangely, it looked as though he were at war with the book. Then he slammed the cover closed. Straightening up, he noticed her watching. There was a raw look of anguish in his eyes, gaping with the vividness of a wound just made. But then it was gone, forced away by will alone. Stiffly, he turned.

"I'll be outside," he said.

Catalina walked to the desk and looked at the book. It was the only book left in the schoolhouse. *Don Quixote.* She'd never heard of it but maybe Paul had. Maybe there was something he hated about it. She picked it up. Dust dulled the cover, and the pages were brittle and rimmed in yellow, but the words were readable. She carried it outside. Paul leaned against a tree, waiting for her. He glanced dully at the book. She put it under her jorongo as quickly as she could.

"I only have one other book," she said, suddenly feeling the need to explain herself.

"Take it." The earnestness in his voice startled her. "You should."

"All right." Warily, she asked, "Have you read it before? *Don Quixote?*"

He said, "I know the story. You'll probably love it. It's a Spanish epic, written by Miguel de Cervantes. Seems like it was meant to find you."

"Really?" Catalina pulled the book out again despite herself and ran her fingers over its cover. The odds of finding a book out here by a Spanish author were slim. It seemed like something from the beyond, a gift from Mamá, to remind her of who she was. She set her satchel down and put it inside.

To her left, Don Pedro cawed. He was flying agitatedly around a nearby tree. Reshouldering her satchel, Catalina walked over to it. A tattered ribbon, the same as the ones tied onto the buildings, was trussed around the tree, as though someone had been afraid it would run away. The ribbon dug cruelly into the bark, cutting deep channels around the trunk, and coppery red fungus spored it. In the fork where the main branches split off, a sheen of rippling veiling hung down and stopped just at eye level with Catalina. Enclaves of brown moths clung to the fabric in clusters, their wings quivering, thin feet stuck in the tiny holes. Though they were trapped, they feasted. Their tiny mouths gnawed on the veil. Catalina stepped back, repulsed.

A soft laugh tittered through the air, and a woman crawled forward from behind the thickest branch on all fours like a scuttling cockroach. The veil hadn't been hanging from the tree like Catalina had first thought. Instead, it was wrapped around the woman's face and Catalina had simply seen its edges.

The veil was secured at her throat and spilled down over her body, which was encased in a cream-colored silk dress as faded as the tablecloths. The hollows of eye and nose sockets pressed against it. A depression formed around the mouth, which was open. It gasped for air but only sucked the veil in closer. Dead rose petals trickled in a crinkly cascade from the neck, and coils of hair grew from her head and wound around her face in thin strands, as tightly as the veiling.

Too late, Catalina saw the woman's arm strike out from beneath the veiling, with a rock clutched in its hand. Catalina only had to time to feel a single moment of panic before the woman struck her over the head. Blackness snapped the world closed around her.

After a bit, images full of vivid colors too bright to exist in nature spun through Catalina's mind. Mamá appeared, wearing a red dress that seemed to float around her. She said something urgent but it was in Spanish, so Catalina couldn't understand, and it felt wrong that she couldn't. Her image cracked open to reveal Pa. Flowers filled his arms and he squinted, unable to see without his spectacles. He didn't say anything. Catalina wanted to apologize to him.

She couldn't remember why, though.

Then Sor Juana was there, wearing a black habit and opening a door. Paul stood next to Sor Juana and seemed to want to go with Catalina but remained in the hall. The door led to a large room where the walls were lined with bookshelves. Dense, angry wilderness scratched at the windows but couldn't get in. Jose Luis sat reading by a crackling fire and Catalina let out a sob of relief.

He smiled and said, "We've been waiting for you. You're home."

Pain burned in a red-hot flame beneath Catalina's scalp, bringing her back to the present. She struggled to open her eyes, seeing the world through blurry slits before managing to open them fully.

She was lying on a lumpy straw mattress, a itchy blanket pulled up to her chin. Atop the blanket was Pa's jacket, the jorongo, and a shirt she recognized as Paul's—they had been tucked over her for extra warmth. The bed was in a farmhouse. Strips of weathered white shiplap ran along the walls, and beams formed bridges inside high rafters.

Paul sat in a chair next to the bed. He was slumped to the side, limbs limp, asleep, ax across his lap.

"Paul?" she croaked, tongue wooden and dry. He stirred but didn't wake. There was a small table by the bed and a tin cup sat atop it, next to her rope belt and Pa's knife. With effort, Catalina pulled her arm from beneath the blanket and cast it over toward the cup. The motion sent her head spinning, but she forced her fingers, numb and distant from her body, to close around the handle. Its edge dragged along the table as she drew it toward herself. At the last minute, she dropped it. The cup clattered to the floor, a thin translucent pool of water flattening across the floorboards.

"Helloooooo!" A voice singsonged from across the room and a woman came along with it, carrying a pitcher. Catalina blinked at her. Two braids hung from her head. They were so long that their tips brushed the floor. Her white hair was as clear as a polished crystal, light glinting in its strands. She wore an ivory dress that seemed as old as she. Shabby bits of lace clung to the skirt and bodice on fragile threads. Her skin reminded Catalina of a crumpled piece of paper that someone had tried to flatten out, covered in wrinkles and lines and pulled tight to her skull.

"Oh, he's still sleeping." The woman dropped her voice to a melodramatic whisper as she approached. "Poor boy was up for two nights by your side. Wouldn't leave you no matter what I said. But you must be thirsty."

Spryly, she snatched up the cup from the floor and poured more water into it. She extended it to Catalina with knobby, puckered hands. Catalina drank it down in two gulps.

"What happened?" Catalina asked, her voice as scratchy as the blanket.

"Oh, you had a run-in with one of my friends. She meant no harm. She just gets jealous when she sees young things like you. Reminds her she's not the blushing bride she used to be."

"Friends? Bride?" Each word took effort, but Catalina forced them out around sharp stabs of pain, futilely attempting to piece together where she was and what had happened. Darkness slithered around the edges of her vision, trying to reclaim her. "Where is this?"

"Welcome to New Appleton," the woman said. "I'm Ruth. Oh, now Jeremiah, don't be such a pest. Go on now. Find your sister and play."

Catalina glanced around. Ruth seemed to be addressing someone in the corner, but only a broom sat in it.

"That's Christianna's son," Ruth said, pointing to the corner. "Always getting into mischief, but all children that age do now, don't they?"

"I . . . I don't see anyone," Catalina rasped. She tried to push herself up onto her elbows. Ruth swept in, propping the pillow up behind her so Catalina could lie back against it.

"No one does at first. But don't you mind. Can you dance? If you can, then you'll have to join us for the wedding tonight. We have one for the bride every time a visitor comes. She gets so distressed if we don't. It's the least you can do, seeing as we saved your life."

"I can't stay. I need to leave. My brother—"

"Paul told me about your brother." Ruth's face sobered. "I'm glad we found you. We are here to warn people like you. People foolish enough to tangle with the Seed Man."

"The Seed Man . . . I think my pa called him the Man of Sap."

"Different names for one evil. Well now." She settled onto the edge of the bed, crisscrossing her braids over her neck, and tossing them over her shoulders. "It never gets easier telling our story, but we do it every time because it's the right thing to do." Despite her burdened expression, Ruth's eyes flashed with excitement, and she eagerly leaned forward, looming like a specter over Catalina.

"Long ago, when I was around your age, I traveled in a wagon party with my parents and several other families. We meant to head out west but came across a promised land filled with apple saplings right here. Instead of continuing, we settled next to them, knowing in several years they would bring us apples. Oh, how thrilled we were. We dreamed of apple wine, apple pie, apple sausages, and apple rosemary chicken."

Dramatically, Ruth rose from the bed and swept across the room. Catalina tried to lean forward so she could nudge Paul awake, feeling anxious as Ruth unspooled her story. Pain radiated through her head in fiery rays. She fell back, pinned to the pillow by the ache.

"The first harvest came after five years, and we thought the trees had been touched by the angels because the apples called to us. Drew us in. We should have known." Ruth wrung her hands and pulled at her braids. "Apples are the fruit of sin, just as they were in Eden. The apples were touched not by angels, but by the Devil. Everyone ate, except for me. Everyone died, except for me. Now, we all live here together and warn people like you. People bent on a mission from Hell. Little do they know who planted the trees—that the Seed Man has cursed the woods from here on out, waking them and filling them with terrible horrors. Things like tree weepers, Hill Gogs, and a White Spider tree—you touch it, and you see a vision of your future—how unnatural! What's more, the Seed Man is more dangerous than ever before. If you even get close to him, it'll be the last thing you do."

"More dangerous?" Catalina's heart pounded, a sharp counterpoint to the pain in her skull. Ruth was peculiar but she knew about the Man of Sap. She might be able to tell her things she didn't know. Things that could help her save Jose Luis.

"Oh yes. The apples love the Seed Man, and they talk about him all the time. They are upset. So upset. He's trying to get out of his deal, you see."

"His deal." Catalina grasped on to the information, desperate to lure more from her host.

"It's how he became cursed in the first place. He made a deal with the banker and regrets it, but it's much too late. The Seed Man will be cursed eternally, just as he deserves."

"You said he made a deal with a banker?"

"Indeed. The fool wanted nothing but fame from growing apple trees, so he sold his soul to get it." Cackling laughter erupted from Ruth and rebounded off the rafters. "Reckon he got more than he realized, but that's what happens when you're willing to give up your soul. Now he's trying to find a way out.

The apples say once his seed sack is empty, he will be free—that's the curse, though. The sack will always fill. The apples will always kill. Now, come! We must see if you can dance. If you can, you'll get to stay for the wedding tonight, then you can head back to where you came from. I'll even give you some of our whiskey. It's one hundred proof, so perhaps only a sip for you. We can't have it any other way, though. Makes us feel alive."

"I'm not heading back." Catalina forced herself to sit up fully, pushing through the swimming currents of pain. She swung her legs over the side of the bed. With her remaining strength, she pulled on Pa's jacket and the jorongo, and managed to slip the rope belt off the table and tie the knife around her waist again. Her satchel sat by the bed, and she hoisted it onto her shoulder. "I'm going on and finding my brother. Now, we came with a bird. Is he around here?"

"Shush with that talk." Sidling up to her, Ruth slipped an arm around her shoulders, gripping her tightly. "I don't want to hear it. Especially when we must see what your dancing is like. We must hurry."

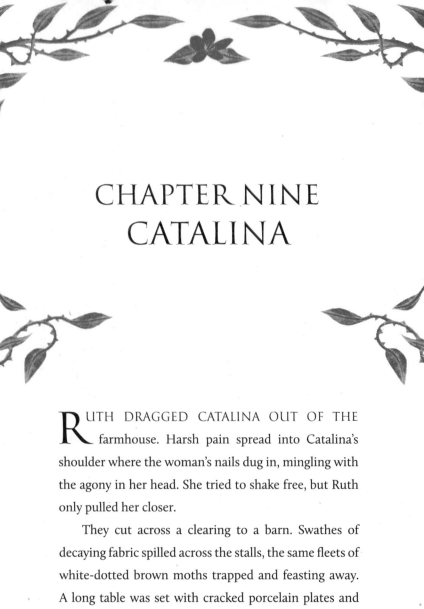

CHAPTER NINE
CATALINA

RUTH DRAGGED CATALINA OUT OF THE farmhouse. Harsh pain spread into Catalina's shoulder where the woman's nails dug in, mingling with the agony in her head. She tried to shake free, but Ruth only pulled her closer.

They cut across a clearing to a barn. Swathes of decaying fabric spilled across the stalls, the same fleets of white-dotted brown moths trapped and feasting away. A long table was set with cracked porcelain plates and adorned with bouquets of dead, papery flowers in jars. Beeswax candles, burned down to drippy stubs, were lit. Even though a heavy patina of stillness sat over the barn, the flames bobbed in an agitated flicker, as though something or someone toyed with the air around them. In the middle of the table was a bulbous cask with a small spout. *Apple Whiskey* was written on the side.

"See now?" Excitement turned Ruth's voice yet another octave higher. "It's all set. Oh, the bride will love it. She'll forgive you for being so, ahem, alive. I just know she didn't mean to hurt you. All right, we must practice so we get the dance just right. As long as you can dance and join the wedding tonight, she'll let bygones be bygones and welcome you with open arms."

Snatching at Catalina's satchel, she tore it from her shoulder and tossed it aside.

"Stop. Let me go." Frantically, Catalina tried to wrest herself from Ruth and grab her knife. But the woman's hold was as unyielding as iron. Her fingers clamped cruelly around Catalina's waist, and she yanked Catalina's arm outward in a dance posture.

"Amos?" Ruth called over her shoulder. "How about some fiddling? We're going to try a square dance."

No music came but Ruth's eyes lit up as though it had. She strode forward and then sideways, dragging Catalina through the steps, singing, "Bum bu bu buuuuummm!" in time to the music that only she heard. Up close, Ruth smelled like rotting flowers and sitting pond water, earthy smells turned grotesque through decay. Fog filled Catalina's brain. She fought against it and inhaled the repellent scents to try to clear her mind.

Jose Luis needed her to get out of here. She would, no matter what.

"Catalina!" Paul's voice came from the barn door. Never had she been so happy to hear him. Relief broke over her like waterlogged clouds finally releasing their rain. She twisted in Ruth's grip to see him leaning against the threshold. Sleep had bedraggled him. His hair and shirt were rumpled into a dishevelment of floppy strands and wrinkled flannel. Blearily, he rubbed his red-rimmed eyes and blinked. "What the hell are you doing?"

"Dancing," Catalina said, stumbling as Ruth picked up the tempo. She noticed his pack was on his back and that his ax was slung over his shoulder. Clearly, he wanted out of here as much as she.

"I can see that. But how is your head? I'm not so sure you should be dancing right now."

"It's a bit of a command perform—"

"We must see if you can dance too!" Ruth screeched. Releasing Catalina, she hurried over to Paul. With a motion as fluid and snappy as a lake eel striking its prey, she grabbed his wrist. He yanked his hand back but, just as Catalina had been, he was helpless. Dragging him forward, Ruth thrust him toward Catalina and pulled his pack off his back. A deep red imprint formed a bracelet around his wrist from where she'd held him. Ruth stationed herself squarely in front of the barn door. Clapping her hands, she called out, "Dance!"

"Well then," Paul said. "Seems like we'll be dancing."

He bowed deeply to Catalina and held out both hands, waiting for her to step into him. She hesitated. Jittery, desperate thoughts of forcing her way past Ruth, finding Don Pedro, and rushing out into the woods ran through her mind.

"May I have this dance?" The words tugged at Catalina. Fury swirled in her at his suggestion to dance when they needed to be escaping. But when she met his eyes, she saw thoughts churning away behind them. She placed one hand on his shoulder, atop the strap that fixed his ax to his back. She slipped the other hand into the one he held out. Something small and fiery and forbidden sparked inside her as his fingers closed around hers. Without pause or an inkling of hesitation, his other hand went to her waist, resting just above the jut of her hip bone. Its warmth spread beneath the fabric of her blouse, a heat that her own skin took on and then made more of, sending a flush through her despite the circumstances. He held her extended hand with the delicacy of an eggshell but the hand on her waist was strong, firm. It felt, suddenly, as though it was the axis of her world, the point on which she spun.

"Dance!" Ruth crowed again and they stepped into the first of the motions. Paul bent over her, his mouth by her ear to say something, and she had a fleeting thought about what it would feel like if he buried his face in the crook of her neck and pressed his lips against her skin.

"That woman is as strong as Hercules," he said. "She's been talking this whole time to people who aren't here. The townsfolk who died, I think."

"She's lost her mind," Catalina whispered back. "After everyone she loved died because of the apples."

Her words seemed to strike Paul hard because he glanced over at Ruth. No animosity or fear tinged his expression. There was only sympathy and sadness, a sadness so strong that Catalina felt its murky depths just looking at him.

"It might be something more." The sadness in his eyes didn't reach his voice. It was clipped and strong. "She wants us to stay for a wedding, but I think her plans go far beyond that."

"Very good!" Ruth's hand disappeared into the folds of her skirt and then reappeared clutching a silvery flask. "Good news.

The bride is pleased with your dancing and wants you to stay for the wedding. Now, let's have a drink. To the wedding and to the bride." She approached, focused on Catalina. "Here, my girl. Now, you must be thirsty. Drink!"

"Stop." In one swift step, Paul came between them. "What is that?"

"Get out of my way, boy." A slow, wicked smile twisted across Ruth's lips. "This isn't for you. You don't need it. The apples told me all about you. Don't worry. You can stay in the farmhouse while you wait. I'll put her corpse next to you while you do, to remind you who will greet you once you cross over. I dug two holes out back. One for you and one for her. Oh, don't look so worried. It'll feel grand to set aside your body. You'll realize how heavy it was, how stifling, itchy, and hot it was."

"What is she talking about?" Catalina gasped.

"Here." In an instant, Ruth shoved Paul aside. Her hand wrapped around the back of Catalina's neck, as tight as a vise. The cold hard metal of the flask rammed against her mouth, bloodying her lips, and clinking hard against her teeth. Paul ran to the banquet table, unsheathing his ax as he did. He jumped atop it. Lifting his ax, he brought it down on the cask. Its blade sliced easily into it, and it broke open like a piece of rotting fruit. Golden red whiskey gushed out onto the table. It surged by the candles, welling up to brush the flames. The minute the flames and liquor met, fire burst across the whiskey in a snakelike blue torrent, spreading to the ribbons and tablecloths.

"No!" Ruth shrieked. She rushed forward, batting at the flames. Paul leapt off the table and grabbed Catalina's hand.

"Hurry!"

They raced to the door but suddenly Ruth appeared in their path.

"You've ruined it." Her face contorted with feral rage and then suddenly veiling, dotted with moths, materialized from behind her skin to rush over her in a cocoon. Dead rose petals fell from her neck and her hair split free of the braids to turn black and wrap around her body. "Just like everyone else who wanted to pick the first apple harvest instead of set up for my wedding and practice their dancing!"

"It's you. You're the bride," Catalina explained.

"I was hanging tablecloths for the wedding and gathering flowers and my supposed friends and family were too desperate to eat apples to help me. Were they starving after our crops failed as we waited for the apples to mature? Yes, but a wedding is new life and transcends our ordinary existences! But they ate the apples and died. So, I hung myself on my veil to find them and have them celebrate with me. And I did! They are all here, all around, all the time. We dance together and celebrate the wedding every night and you must join us, forever."

The table collapsed in a crash behind them, sending angry sparks spiraling through the air. Flames crawled along the stalls and beams, pitching higher and higher toward the rafters. Ruth screamed and plunged back toward the table. She grabbed a feed sack and fought against the flames, desperately trying to subdue them.

With Ruth distracted, Catalina and Paul fled. Outside, the fire engulfed the barn. Jagged flames leapt higher and higher as though needing more to devour than just the barn. A realization struck Catalina, one more soul-searing than any fire could ever be. She turned back.

"My satchel! The books!"

She wasn't even certain Paul heard her over the bellow of the fire. In fact, she hadn't even been talking to him. The exclamation had come from the depths of her heart, spoken simply because it was too much to hold inside. But he had, because he jerked to a stop beside her, looked from her to the barn, and then rushed back inside.

CHAPTER TEN
CATALINA

CATALINA STARED INTO THE BARN. IT seemed to thrash before her as the flames raged through it. Rafters began to collapse. She clamped her hands over her mouth in horror. What had Paul done? The barn was an inferno. Icy cold terror, as strong as the heat, stabbed through her heart.

Paul burst from the burning barn, clutching her satchel. It was on fire. He cast it down and stomped out the flames, violently coughing. With a gasp, he threw himself onto the grass next to it.

"Are you all right?" Catalina knelt by his side, impulsively grabbing his hand.

"How's the satchel?" he asked through fits of short, choking coughs.

"You shouldn't have done that! It was too dangerous." Slowly, she touched his face and wiped soot off his forehead. He ducked his head and nodded toward the satchel.

"Is it all right?"

"No, first tell me you're not dying."

"Too late for that," he said in an oddly lifeless tone that cut against the coughs. "I've heard we start dying the moment we are born. Important thing is the books."

Catalina turned to the satchel. It was hot. She pulled Pa's jacket down over her hands to protect her fingers and flipped it open. A cloud of throat-stinging smoke hit her in the face. Staring inside, she let out a quavering breath. The books were blackened into misshapen rectangles. The pages were shriveled, curling into themselves, and burned practically beyond recognition. Catalina's fingers were weak and boneless within the cuffs of the jacket as she lifted out Mamá's book. She hadn't cried when Pa died. She hadn't cried when Jose Luis had been taken. But clutching the remains of Mamá's book, her throat and eyes burned, as though the fire had come alive in them. She could hold the book, but the words were destroyed. *Mamá's handwriting was destroyed.* The book was singed black and smoking, a thing devoid of its soul and meaning.

A scream came from the barn. Catalina heard it in a remote part of her brain. The bride.

"We need to go," Paul gasped.

He struggled to his feet and they stumbled away. Their steps were halting. Catalina held the book in her hand, knowing in her heart that the item that made her feel closest to Mamá was gone.

As they fled, shadows lengthened around them, shifting anxiously and then springing up as though suddenly cut free.

Catalina let out a frightened cry as pairs of eyes materialized in the air. Faces filled in around the eyes, then bodies, until several people surrounded them. The townsfolk. They were riddled with the same red marks Catalina had seen on Pa. You could see right through them, yet they were there, wispy outlines of long-gone souls. Silently, they looked at Catalina and Paul before turning to stare at the inferno. Their eyes and bodies reflected the flames, so they seemed to be on fire too.

Catalina and Paul kept going. Even as they put space between them and New Appleton, bits of ash swirled on the breeze and an orangey glow draped heavy over the tree line. Crackles, pops, and hisses echoed from New Appleton and, through it all, they could still hear screams from the bride.

"Whole town is on fire," Paul said grimly. A fit of coughing overtook him, and he stopped, bracing himself against a tree. Eventually, he slid down it to sit. After the coughing spell passed, his face was white. Catalina realized her own head swam. The anesthetic of adrenaline was passing, and her hurts awakened in fierce force. Woozily, she sank down next to him.

"Don Pedro is gone," she said. "And we have no supplies."

She stared at the burned book in her hands. The only things left were Paul's ax and Pa's knife. They were as stranded as a ship in the middle of an ocean. Panic consumed her, devouring every rational thought. The trees seemed to press in on every side, as endless as the sky but as confining as a prison. How could she find Jose Luis now? This entire time, she'd been able to find action in loss, strength to throw off the cruel, suffocating wiles of the world. But now, everything was gone, burned to nothing like the corpse of Mamá's book.

Pulling her knees to her chest, she wrapped her arms around them. She'd lost him. Her brother. She'd failed him. The stabbing pain in her chest grew, the emotional pain so strong it made the physical pain dull by comparison. She understood the bride better now. Why she would linger there, talking to memories as though they were the people she'd lost to the apples.

The apples.

Catalina returned to Pa's stories once again, to the bits of information buried inside them like seeds of their own. Once you took a bite, John stood by your side and watched as you died. The bride had said there were trees outside of New Appleton. She'd also said that if John's bag were emptied of seeds, he'd be free from his curse. Would that make him mortal? Catalina's hand went to the knife at her side.

Maybe she could find one of John's trees. Take an apple and take a bite. Then John would come . . . *no.* How could she help her brother if she was dead? Don Pedro had been leading them deeper into these woods. John was somewhere here—had to be— if they just pressed on.

"We should look for water," she said to Paul, standing. "You need some. Then we must keep going."

Sweat ran through the soot on Paul's face, dragging dirty tracks down it. He nodded exhaustedly and, with effort, pushed himself to his feet. Catalina wiped her eyes with the edge of the jorongo and stared down at the charred book. Then she threw it onto the ground.

"Wait," Paul protested. "Don't just throw it away."

"I don't want it." Mouth set, she started off at a brisk pace, even though each step made the pain in her head worse.

"But you do. It belonged to your mamá. It's one of the only things you have left of her."

Every word Paul said was true and each one seemed to reverberate in the hollow of her chest, repeating over and over so she could not unhear them or stop the pain that they drew from her. She spun around, pointing at him.

"Don't tell me what it is to me. I know, and it's gone. Just like everyone I've ever cared about." She caught herself. "You're the last person who would understand. You're out here gallivanting through the woods, and for what? Money? Glory? So don't tell me what my things mean to me because you have no idea how something can hurt you so much by just existing, like the book and—you don't understand at all."

"Stop." Fury lit Paul's eyes, blazing as ferociously as the fire consuming New Appleton. "You don't get it as much as you think you do."

"I know you're a little boy playing a game who can go home anytime he wants." She was being cruel now, much too cruel, but she didn't care.

"Go home? What home?"

"To . . ." She knew he wasn't close with his father. Still, he must have some place where he belonged. "What about your mother?"

"Gone. Just like yours. But you never stopped to realize someone else might have suffered too, might *be* suffering."

He was right. All she'd been focusing on was how he was out here for no good reason, as though his choices were hers to judge. "I didn't realize she'd passed away."

"Died when I was born. In childbirth."

"Oh." Jose Luis had so few real recollections of Mamá. Catalina was always trying to give him hers, quilting them into his memories so he could feel Mamá's warmth and how she'd kept their little family stitched together with love. "Did your father tell you about her?"

The question was meant to make amends, but Paul's lips twisted in a grimace and his eyes went empty. "Maybe water is this way," he said, pushing past her.

Without thought, she grabbed his arm. He let her draw him to a stop and stared down at her in silence. Her hand slid down to his wrist. "I don't mean to pry," she said. "Jose Luis doesn't have many memories of Mamá so I try to tell him everything I remember. I know you aren't close to your father, but I was thinking maybe he did the same or someone else in your family did."

"You're a good sister." The sincerity in Paul's voice only made her feel worse.

"But a bad friend, it would seem."

"Now that's true." A hint of playfulness lifted the flatness of his tone. "Don't worry about it. I'm tough."

With a start, Catalina realized she was still holding his wrist and she could feel his pulse gently thrumming away. She let him go. Ducking her head, she started walking again and he caught up to her.

"Thank you for trying to save the books," she said.

"Anytime." He shrugged as though running into a burning barn for books was as significant as milking a cow.

"Maybe later on you can tell me what happens in *Don Quixote*, since you've read it." She wished to make amends but was uncertain as to how.

"Well, I never actually read it myself. Just memorized some of the chapters."

"Wait." Catalina frowned. "How did you memorize chapters if you didn't read it?"

"I . . ." He hesitated, and she saw him swallow, hard. Then, slowly, he said, "My father had a servant to run the house after my mother died. She overheard the lessons my father gave me and learned to read herself. Then she read it to me along with other classics. I memorized it that way to appease him. Make him think I could read."

Of all things, this was the last she'd expected. Plenty of people didn't know how to read and write but he was the son of a school-teacher and had just said his father gave him lessons. "What do you mean? I thought your father taught you."

"He tried. But words move all over the page for me. They flip and jumble and turn around so most of the time I'm guessing at what they say. When I write, it's the same thing."

Catalina thought about words. How they were combina-tions of the same twenty-six letters. How she knew each one at the merest glance. What would it be like if they moved about, as though the page were water through which they swam? She thought about Paul bent over the book in the schoolhouse, brow furrowed as he stared at the pages, and how he'd slammed the cover shut.

"You must see things differently."

"Or I'm just stupid." He stared off into the woods as they trudged along. By now, they'd walked far enough to escape the reach of ash. Only the thick smoky smell remained. It coated Catalina's tongue and the inside of her nose, an acrid note to underscore Paul's words. "That's what my father said once he realized I was memorizing the books and not reading them. Took me to eye doctors and head doctors. If he'd known I wouldn't be able to read, he would've left me in a basket on a doorstep when I was born. All came to a head one day when he said I was like my mother. Simple. That it was her fault I'm . . . the way I am, and I hit him. So hard it knocked him out."

The anger left his face, but the sadness stayed. Grew, until it filled up his eyes and all she wanted was to make it go away. She could see it even as he stared resolutely forward, his steps heavy. "When he came to, he said he always knew I was a dumb brute. I left then. Got a job in logging. Figured I should put my strength to use because Lord knows I'll never do anything with my mind. But every day as I felled logs, it was like he was there, staring at me in disgust and saying I'd proven him right."

"That's terrible," Catalina said. She paused and he followed her lead. They faced each other. "I'm sorry."

"Not your fault."

"It's more than that. I've been unkind."

"Aside from stabbing me, it really hasn't been too bad." His boyish grin hovered on his tired face. "I've hated books for a long time now, but seeing the way you look at them has been, well, nice. Maybe you should try to write one, someday."

"I don't know. I used to write poetry. But I haven't in a long while. Mamá's poetry book is—was—by Sor Juana de la Cruz, who was a poet and a nun. When I read her poems, they made me feel alive, like I was breathing a different type of air. I felt that way when I wrote them too."

"Tell me one."

"What?"

"One of your poems. I'm sure you know one by heart. Can I hear it?"

"They aren't very good." The flush in her cheeks darkened from pink to red. "I couldn't."

"Just one. It'll help pass the time as we look for water."

Catalina thought about Sor Juana and Mamá. Maybe she would. Not for herself, but for them. And for Jose Luis, who always leaned against her shoulder while she wrote poetry. She'd recite it then put it and the rest away, in the drawer of her mind. She began walking again, because there certainly was no way she could just stand there saying it, and he joined her, head tilted toward her to hear. Clearing her throat, she began.

"The trees are an ocean

And our cabin is a boat

Trying to get to the island sun above.

Before we get there,

You wish to walk among the treetops

And step outside the boat.

But it was water and you sank—"

The rest of the lines caught in her throat, and she stopped.

"I don't remember the rest," she lied. Stuffing her hands into her pockets, she stared at the tips of her dusty shoes as they plodded along. Saying the poem aloud was like taking her heart out of her chest and holding it out for everyone to see, even if *everyone* was only Paul. And hearts weren't pretty. At least, hers wasn't. It was a bloody, pulsing thing that beat with pain and was shaded in angry, grief-stricken red and rotting, despairing black.

She'd always told herself that poems kept you from facing the present. But there was more. Poems made you face your life in all its entirety, the whole timeline of good and bad. Her words took their breaths from her dreams and losses. They were full of them, sustained by them. And there'd been more losses than dreams, so many more that the dreams seemed to have drifted away. Why hadn't she recited a different poem or, for that matter, none at all? This one was about Mamá and was full of the hurt that welled from her heart. She wished she could take it back.

"Anyway, I'm certain it doesn't qualify as a poem," she spoke quickly, trying to recenter herself. "Poems have rules. Metrics and beats. I don't know what they are, but I wish I did."

"It's good, Catalina. Really good."

Her hands, fisted inside her pockets, uncurled at his encouragement. She closed them again. It was what she knew to do. Stay closed, guarded, doors and windows of her soul closed to keep herself safe.

Then something off to the side caught her eye. She stopped, stared. Everything else was forgotten. For a moment, she didn't dare believe it.

But there it was.

One of John's trees.

CHAPTER ELEVEN
JOHN

THAT FIRST NIGHT AFTER SEEING THE GIRL die from eating my apples lasted forever.

And I know what forever is. I live it now. As it is, my life is a book with no ending, just chapter after chapter. All of them full of the same words and read by only me. But as I huddled among the trees and stared up at the bangle of stars overhead, guilt raged over me like a fever. Daybreak eventually spilled its yellow ink into the sky, and I looked dully up at it, stunned that a new day was beginning. The night had been so consuming, so vivid, so agonizing that something as ordinary as the morning's gentle sunshine no longer seemed possible. Not for me.

I picked myself up. Continued. But since I now knew the full weight of my consequences, the joy and meaning I'd found in planting was gone. My trees were alive, yes, but they caused death. While the strap dug into my shoulder, this knowledge dug into me. Burrowed like a poisonous tick that could never be extricated, and even the laud from the agricultural community, universities, and government couldn't ease it.

And, in the most secret part of me, I mourned because my gift of fecundity came hand in hand with death and destruction.

Once my trees started bearing fruit and eager people ate from them, I was pulled to their deaths. Sometimes, when many people ate them, time would suspend, and I'd walk from one to the next. Every sort of person lay at my feet. Adults. Children. Rich, poor, everyone in between. My apples called to all equally and destroyed all equally. I received their last words, their last gazes as they left the only world they'd known. Some feebly tried to touch my Bible and whisper scriptures, some fumbled with amulets at their necks and spoke to the great spirits, some called for their children or parents or lovers. Others merely stared at me, bewildered, terrified, fighting for one more minute, one more second, one more millisecond. As it happened, over and over, the red birds sang their doleful song and the trees whispered in satisfaction and asked if they made me proud.

The birds followed me. They tried to nest in my hair, sit on my shoulders, and peck up the bugs that had made me their home. After they started tearing out my hair to make nests, I found a rusted pot and wore it on my head for protection. No matter how quickly I moved or tried to lose them, they found me.

Like my curse, I could never be rid of them.

Eventually, I was in a hell like the one described in Marguerite's Bible, which I wore tucked into my belt at my waist. Scenes of death played out before me; tableaus reset with new players stricken with a single fate. Pain racked my body. My shame and loneliness were so strong that they sometimes brought me to my knees.

It needed to end. Once I knew that and what to do about it, some manner of peace settled upon me. I'd found the only human part of me left. The will to stop it. For several nights, I holed up in an abandoned farmhouse and wrote my final conclusions on apple cultivation. My resolve weakened and I could barely make myself post it to my contact at the horticultural society because I truly did love trees and sharing my knowledge on apple farming.

But I had to let go.

Steeling myself, I tied one of the red ribbons Marguerite wore to our wedding around my wrist and went to the high mountainous wilds of West Virginia. A cluster of my trees grew there. No one had ever eaten from them because they were atop a mountain. In fact, apple trees had no business up there. It was much too cold and even in late May, snow still covered the ground. Glittering white powder dusted the heads of my trees, making them look like silent, old giants in green robes. My birds flew to them, shaking them awake. The trees shook off their snowy coats and leaned toward me, whispering, calling me *father*.

"Are you proud of us?" they asked. *"Do we please you?"*

I didn't hesitate. I plucked one of the apples. My trees cried out *"Father! No!"* My birds opened their wings and screamed. Most likely, the banker would come and drag me to Hell, where Marguerite said I belonged. God knew I deserved it.

I leaned on the nearest tree, feeling its bark and my own creak against each other in a final song, and said, "I love you."

Then I took a bite.

※

I awoke slowly, slumped in a chair, forehead pressed to a tabletop. The last thing I remembered was biting my apple. Ever since the curse, any food I tried to eat was tasteless and dusty in my mouth.

But not my apple.

It had rolled over my tongue in notes. Pure sweetness followed by the sort of crispness you find in mountain air and, lastly, a decadence as heady and rich as a rarified port. As I chewed, I felt the way I had when I saw my Gabriel for the first time, like the wrongs in my life had been strangely righted when his tiny fingers wrapped around my finger, like there was a reason why I was here.

Then the taste changed. It turned to ash on my tongue and fire in my stomach. My skin blistered up through the cracks in my bark. The sap in my eyes congealed into an oily, burning acid. I'd collapsed.

With effort, I forced myself up from the table and looked around. I was inside a cabin. It gently listed from side to side as though it were on water. Branches grew through the center of it, and one of them was hollowed out to form a fireplace. It was lit and a kettle hung over the blaze.

"You're up!" Holding two mismatched teacups, the banker strolled over from the far side of the room. "Here. Coffee. It'll make you right as rain."

He handed me one of the teacups. I was so surprised, I took it, even though I wouldn't drink it. Dazed, I placed it on the table and looked down. Bark still encased my body, but the blisters were gone and though my head ached and the sack hung from my shoulder, I didn't feel too bad.

"Where . . . where am I?"

"This is your new home. Fantastic, isn't it?" Home. For the past decade, I'd had no home aside from the ground I'd lain on at night. "By the way, how are those white teeth treating you? Pretty spectacular, don't you think?"

"Is this Hell?"

At the word *Hell*, the banker's eyes flashed with pleasure, as though he'd just heard the strain of a beloved song or taken a sip of his favorite whiskey.

"Yes, this is Hell itself. I made it just for you, back when you first signed your contract."

I bent over the table until my forehead pressed against it again, a new despair sinking into my hollows. Marguerite had been right. I'd tried to escape, but Hell had waited for me and now it had me. I realized her Bible was gone.

"We have some things to discuss." Suspicion niggled at me. The banker's smile was much too big, his voice much too loud. He was inching toward something. Something bad. "You ate one of your apples, killing yourself and letting me collect the body you've been walking around in for the past decades. However, I still need you to plant. I'll send you out from time to time to do so."

"You will still make me plant?"

The banker shrugged apologetically, and my panic turned to anger. Knocking over the table in front of me, I jumped up and ran at him, pinning him to the wall. I held him there, my arm across his throat. Surprise engulfed his face, followed by a smile that cut across his face so sharply, it could've been etched there by a knife. He waved his hand. A bolt of lightning surged through me in an electric zing of pain. I was thrown across the room. I landed in a heap against the wall, shedding leaves and bark across the floor.

"Don't try me, impudent boy." Towering over me, I thought he might tear me limb from limb. Then he took two breaths. The first breath was furious but the second one seemed to cool the fire of its predecessor and calm him. Meticulously, the banker brushed off his suit and ran a hand through his hair. "Do you think I just want you here, rotting away with no use to me? When your trees spread pain faster than any of my other debtors have the ability to?"

I went limp against the wall. I'd done it again. Made things worse. I would still be forced to plant, only this time with no choice, no agency. I touched the strap of my bag, running my fingers along its scratchy length as though I could simply take it off.

"It's hard to wish you were something you aren't," the banker said, not unkindly. "Long ago, I did fancy myself a creator. Look out the window, Johnny."

I clambered stiffly to my feet. The banker returned to the table and took a seat but seemed to know exactly what I was seeing. The sight outside the window was as suffocating as a pillow over the face. The cabin was about thirty feet off the ground, cradled in the branches of a tree. More trees stretched out around it as far as the eye could see, every single one laden with apples. Above, claustrophobically close, a miasma of earth and atmosphere seemed to mix in a lurid reddish haze. Roots poked through it, hanging down as though we were in the underside of a grave. They hung in limp tendrils. I hadn't registered it before, but it was warm, stiflingly so. Heat settled into the glass on the window, enough to make the panes too hot to touch. There was the sound of water. A creek slashed its way across the ground.

"A water element," the banker said. "It really adds to the layout of the place, don't you think? Just don't drink it . . . and maybe don't look too closely."

At that, I squinted. A white shape lurked beneath the water. It broke through the surface. I gasped. It was a fish, but it had two heads on either end. The heads struggled to swim in opposite directions. They swam so vigorously they slowly tore apart in the middle. Streamers of blood trailed from it, mixing with the water.

"So you see," the banker said. "The things I touch . . . well, let me show you."

He held up his hands. To my shock, his fingertips sparked, and smoke emitted from them in long, vaporous shafts. It grew thick and dark before drifting away. A small creature was in his hands. It was a cross between a cat and a rat, yet its incisors were of a much larger animal.

Something else was amiss. I leaned closer. Pinkish liquid leaked from its mouth. Fighting to breathe, it trembled in the banker's hands.

The banker whispered quietly back to it and then, with one quick motion, broke its neck. The sound was akin to someone flexing their knuckles. He brought it to his lips and gently kissed its head. When he looked up, tears were in his eyes.

"I made it." His voice was old and tired. Still holding the creature with one hand, he ran the other through his hair, for once disheveling it. "Now I cannot unmake it. It's part of this world. It'll decay and rot and turn to dust, but some part of it will always be here. Sometimes, this power has been useful. I've been renowned in many kingdoms for my 'plagues.' But I don't like to use it. It reminds me of what I am not and what I hoped to be, making creatures fit for only death."

"If you make them, maybe you should care for them," I said dully.

At that, he laughed, as hard as he had when I'd told him I wanted my orchard to prosper all those years ago. I cringed, unable to control my horror. This laughter was vicious, contorting his face as much as the sound. It was pure evil, right there before me. Not a secondary or inherited evil. But the sort that started it all, the first crack that shattered the world so that everyone carries its slivers.

CATALINA

There was no way to mistake John's tree. It was vivid against the woods, dominating the landscape as though the sky, earth, and sun existed for it alone.

Its shape made Catalina think of an upright hand reaching from the soil, the trunk a wrist, the branches fingers. Irrationally, she thought that this hand wasn't open to give—it was open to take, and it deserved all and more that the world could give. It made her feel as though she had some small part to play in its purpose and would willingly give herself to it, if it just told her how to do so.

The tree's trunk was a honeyed amber streaked with crystal-line rivers. Golden leaves created a luminous corona around it. Even from her distance, Catalina saw that the leaves were made of delicate fibers. They braided together and hung on the tree like a gossamer gown.

A bounty of apples dangled from each branch, a collection of charms just waiting to be plucked. They were so deep red that, at first, Catalina thought they were black. But that wasn't right. They were dark red, a shade deeper than blood. With a start, she recognized them. She'd first seen them sitting in a row of three across the threshold of the cabin.

"Can you hear them?" Paul asked hoarsely. Catalina tore her eyes from the tree to look at Paul. His face was pinched, his brow drawn as though whatever he heard pained him.

"Hear what?"

"The apples. You don't hear them whispering? Telling you to come and eat?"

Catalina frowned, cocking her head to the side. "I don't . . . Paul!"

He staggered past her, toward the tree. His hand lifted from his side and his fingers grasped through the air. One of the apples glowed bright as he approached. It reflected him, capturing his visage in its starry surface. The branch unwound like a snake. It slithered through the air.

"Stop!" Terror rushed her to his side. She slapped his hand down and yanked him around so his back was to the tree. "It's luring you in."

His weight crushed against her, and they collapsed to the ground in a heap of limbs. Catalina pulled him upward, so he leaned against her and they sat side by side. His breath came fast and strangled. It skipped across her face, hot and desperate.

"Paul?"

Paul frowned, as though hearing her from a distance. His eyes danced around but eventually they came to focus on her face and he shook his head. Underneath his tan, his face was white, drawn.

"It almost got me," he said. A shuddering breath passed through his body.

"Well, it didn't." Slightly unsure, she pushed his hair back from his forehead. It was sweaty and stood up in tufts. Her hand wanted to return to it, but she lowered it. "What's it like?"

"Feels almost like a string. Like you've been barbed on a fisherman's line and you know it's drawing you to your death, but you *want* to go. You don't hear it? Not at all?"

Catalina dared to glance over her shoulder at the tree. It had no eyes, yet it seemed as though it stared back at her. Shivers shook her at the knowledge it was danger and death. But she heard no whispers beyond the wind stirring the leaves into a dance. No string pulled her forward and her hands remained limp at her sides, unbidden.

"No." She kept staring. "Though I didn't realize it would be so beautiful."

John, in the small glimpses she'd seen of him, was terrifying. A distorted duality of man and nature. Nothing beautiful or enticing about him. But this tree traced back to him, his hands planted it and brought it to life. How could something so beautiful come from someone so fearsome?

Paul pushed himself to his feet, his back still to the tree. He waited a few moments until his breath was completely recovered and some color resurfaced on his cheeks. Then he unsheathed his ax. Turning around, he hurried to the tree, stopping to take a wide stance in front of it. His head tilted up at his foe and despite his strength, he seemed defenseless against the tree. Unsure.

"Watch out!" Catalina cried as one of the branches swiped at him. It was enough to make him explode into motion. The ax cut through the air and struck the trunk. It bit. Deep.

Catalina heard it then. A silky whispering that ran around the woods like a mockingbird repeating its own ridicules. Only it quickly turned high-pitched, discordant, shrill. Paul wrenched the ax free, and the blade dripped with a red-gold liquid. He struck it again and the tree trembled, its leaves unfolding and refolding, its apples becoming brighter with each passing second. Even though she knew it had to be done, Catalina had the inexplicable urge to tell him to stop, that the tree was hurting.

Paul paused but it wasn't to stop. It was to catch his breath. Shakily, he wiped his arm across his brow. He lifted the ax and struck the tree so hard the red and gold liquid splattered across his face, arms, and chest. The high-pitched whispering grew to an anguished shriek and Catalina shook, just as the tree was shaking.

On the third blow, a bizarre *thunk* rang out and the trunk split open. A noxious wind gushed out of it, smelling of rot and poison. Catalina gasped. The tree was hollow inside and spotted with white patches of furry decay. The decay moved. Released from the innards of the tree, it spread. The delicate, lacelike leaves disintegrated at its touch and the apples dropped from the branches, as though trying to escape. The ones that didn't drop glowed an even brighter red before exploding into pieces that hung from the branches like shredded entrails.

Every inch of Catalina's skin crawled, and she wanted to cover her eyes. Once, years ago, she'd seen a songbird overwhelmed by fire ants. The tiny specks of red roved over its body and into its eyes and, despite that she'd seen all manner of nature's brutality, she was sick to her stomach. The sight of the tree being eaten by its own rot was worse.

Paul kept going. Even though his chest heaved, he kept swinging and, with each connection of his ax to the tree, the rot spread faster until it was nothing more than a reeking pile. The only evidence of what it had been was the vague, lingering fragrance and the few apples that had plummeted to the ground.

One of apples rolled a small distance. It came to a stop at Catalina's feet.

He watches while you die.

The idea she'd dismissed before came back. Take the apple. Bite it. Summon John. She knew the plan was too desperate, too dangerous. Still, this whole trip had been desperate and dangerous. It might be wise to have it, just in case. Out of the corners of her eyes, she glanced at Paul. He was immersed in felling the tree, but still, she needed to be careful. Sinking down, she let her skirt cover the apple and picked it up. It was cold and glassily smooth. Quickly, she dropped it into her pocket, where it sat atop Pa's spectacle rims. She buttoned the top two buttons closed.

The rotting heap collapsed in on itself, a final surrender to its end. Paul crushed the remaining apples under his heel, grinding them into bits. They burst into sinewy shreds like the others. The shrill keening died. It was over.

Weakly, Paul took a bandana from his pocket and wiped his ax blade clean. He put the ax into its sheath and slung it over his back. His breath came in desperate gulps and his brow dripped with sweat. He lowered himself to the ground. The muscles in his forearms throbbed, jumpy from the exertion. Around breaths, he said, "Something always bothers me about cutting down trees, but not John's trees."

"You'd never know there was so much rot inside." Catalina's voice was too high. The apple was heavy in her pocket, but the jacket was thick enough to hide it.

"The tree is a creature of prey," Paul said. "Its beauty lures you in."

"We should keep going. Don Pedro was flying in this direction." She pointed but it was hard to focus, even on her own words. The apple in her pocket was cold, so cold it numbed her thigh through her layers of clothes. No matter. She was glad she had it, just in case.

The apple rubbed against Catalina's thigh with every step, prying against her, sending its coolness deeper into her skin. She might not be able to hear its call, but that didn't prevent her from feeling its effects. Soon, her leg was numb. She wasn't the only one struggling. Paul moved even slower than before. It only got worse as the terrain slithered upward in an incline, the trees growing against gravity and one half of the ground peeling away from the other. Soon, they were walking along a narrow ledge of space between the trees and a drop-off pockmarked with rocks and brush.

A fat raindrop hit her cheek. She touched it, confused. Overhead, though the daylight was tinged with the coming gray of fall, there wasn't a single cloud to be seen. Another followed, splatting across her brow in an explosion of water, salt, and the rich scent of jasmine. It hung gelatinously on her brow as though mixed with oil.

"What on earth—" she asked, just as Paul said, "Look!"

He pointed to a tree. A woman sat high in its branches in a sheer pinkish-gray gown with a long train that tumbled almost to the ground. It was drenched, plastered to her body. Her shoulders shook and her hands covered her face, along with wet tendrils of hair. No wails or sobs could be heard, but she seemed to be weeping and all around her, rain fell.

"Do you think it's her tears?" Catalina whispered, staring at the woman.

"Ruth said the apples woke all sorts of things," Paul said. "She must be a tree weeper."

They passed beneath her weeping rain. Her tears fell fast and hard. Not once did she raise her head or acknowledge them. Catalina breathed a sigh of relief once she was behind them. In this cursed wood of haunts and horrors, you never knew what to expect. They'd only just passed her when three more appeared perched on the branches of trees up ahead. The first one wore a dark green dress and the other two wore soft lavender gowns and leaned against each other. Their hair seemed to mix into one. All of them were soaked and tears dripped from their hems onto the ground in a steady *plip plop.*

Catalina assumed the trio also wouldn't notice them, and the entangled tree weepers didn't. But the third suddenly jumped down, landing frog-like in front of them.

"Get back!" Catalina said as rain came down around them. "Shoo!"

"I think it might be trying to tell you something," Paul said. It was true. The tree weeper hopped forward on bended legs, arms extended straight down in front. Her waterlogged dress was much too long but it pushed up over her knees. She lifted her hand, which was a webbed paw. Catalina stared into her huge, black-blue eyes. They seemed to swim with water, and there were furrows down her cheeks following the path tears would naturally take—but there were no actual tears. Instead, rain fell around the tree weeper, splattering Catalina as well. These drops had a hint of pepper and citrus mixed with brine.

"We are looking for the Man of Sap," Catalina said, drawn into the endless, watery pools of the tree weeper's eyes. "Can you help?"

Gently, the tree weeper hopped forward and looked over her shoulder, expectantly.

"Are we supposed to follow every creature in the world?" Catalina muttered. First Don Pedro, now the tree weeper.

"Can't hurt," Paul said. "Maybe they know where he's at."

The tree weeper didn't take them far. They walked in her rain, drops splattering their faces and making Catalina long all the more for fresh water. Stopping abruptly, the tree weeper pointed with one of her paws. Straight ahead was a tree. But it wasn't one of John's trees. This one seemed to be a pine tree, leached of all its color so it was an anemic white. Its branches wrapped tightly around it and the upper part of the tree bent forward, as though it was in a deep sleep. Thousands of spiderweb silks spun around it. If Catalina hadn't realized it was spiderwebs, the tree would've looked delightful, like it was covered in skeins of fleecy white yarn or heads of dandelion fluff. Two tree weepers sat in its branches. Their tears caught on the silks and shivered on them like hundreds of pearls.

The tree weeper leading Catalina let out a keening wail. The tree startled awake, and the tree weepers leapt off as it straightened with a loud creak. Five eyes, grouped in the center of the trunk, slid open. They were red with a black ellipse in the center. The eyes didn't swivel once. Every single one immediately centered on Catalina.

"The White Spider tree," Catalina gasped. "Ruth said you touch it and see a vision from your future."

"Are you going to try?" Paul asked, warily watching the tree.

"I . . ." She stared back at the five eyes. At this point, there wasn't much of a choice. She didn't know where to go or what to do to save Jose Luis. "Yes, I am. Are you?"

"Naw. Don't need to."

Catalina understood his reluctance. Slowly, cautiously, she inched closer. One branch opened and protracted out, long silks hanging beard-like from it, seeming to invite her to lay her hand down. Maybe she shouldn't. What if she saw something terrible in the vision? But she had to. There might be a clue.

Her hand hovered over it and she wasn't certain she could do it. Before her resolve abandoned her completely, she forced her palm flat against the branch.

An image flashed sharp in the White Spider tree's eyes, as clear as a painting and as vivid as a nightmare. In it, a single tree stood tall against a red, inflamed sky. Three bodies hung from it by ropes tied around their waists. They bent at the middle, heads cast back, arms and legs hanging limply in the air. Slits cut leering smiles around their necks and blood stained their clothing.

Quick as a flash, the image was gone.

"Wait!" Catalina cried. "Bring it back! What does it mean?"

But in her heart, she knew. It was a tree with her, Paul, and Jose Luis. The sight made her woozy and weak. What sort of monster did such a thing? She knew. The Man of Sap. She stumbled back from the White Spider tree, even as she wanted to see the image again so she could understand it, undo it, fix it.

"What did you see?" Paul asked.

"I saw . . ." She struggled for air, even though it was all around her. "I saw us, dead in a tree."

"I see." Thoughtfully, Paul ran his hand along his jaw. "Dead or asleep?"

"Dead, Paul," she snapped. She sank to her knees and rubbed her eyes as though she could wipe away the image. "Dead as can be. Throats slit."

"Got it." He knelt next to her. "Don't doubt it. All I'm saying is that maybe the tree shows one possibility. You never know. As it is, your only choices are to go back or keep going forward. Do you want to keep going, even if that's what waits?"

"Keep going." If anything, the vision made her more desperate to find her brother. She would do everything she could to save him from this future. If it was written, set, a road on which they had no choice but to walk, she would die next to him.

The White Spider sank back into sleep. There was nothing to do but keep going. Catalina's steps were nearly as heavy and slow as Paul's, hers weighted by doom and his by illness. Both were afflicted with thirst. Her throat was so dry, it felt as though sun-bleached kindling filled the back of it. They needed to find a river or a creek. Fast.

Eventually, Paul held up a hand.

"I think there's water. Listen."

"Up ahead," Catalina agreed dully. Her eyes narrowed as she examined his face. "Are you sure you should keep going?" He'd struggled this whole time, the effects of the cholera working against his youthful strength and slowly turning him inside out.

"Still trying to get rid of me?"

"No. But I'm worried about you."

"You're worried about me? It's all right. I'm going to die next to you in a tree." His attempt at a joke didn't work. She pulled Pa's jacket tightly across her chest, cringing at the thought. Most would abandon humor at that point, but he was undeterred. "Though I imagine you might not like that. Remember, you hate me for my vainglory."

It was enough to make her loosen, just a bit. "I suppose you have every right do what you wish," she said slowly. "I don't want to be here, so it's hard to understand someone who does, especially when it's costing you so much and there's things like, well, a tree with our dead bodies looming in the immediate future. But I'm glad you're here."

"Are you?" He glanced at her with a strange, sad surprise.

"I am. And I'm sorry I was so callous about your father earlier."

"The tree vision made you go soft," Paul teased. "Making amends in case we're about to die?"

"No, I assumed things about you when I shouldn't have." She bit the inside of her lip. Seeing the White Spider's tree vision made her think about endings. Specifically, about how things had ended with

Pa. "Honestly, I carry my own regrets. When Pa died . . ." She trailed off. She wasn't certain she could finish. Jose Luis was the one who expressed emotion for them both. The one who loved and lost as Catalina couldn't because she had to be strong. But maybe there was more to it. Maybe she was afraid of life. After seeing so much bad, the good seemed like a threat, something to be turned against you.

"I took his spectacles off, a day before the end. He was restless and I was worried they would break. I thought it wouldn't matter because he wasn't very lucid but—" She tightened her grip on the jacket. Not to reassure him but to steady herself. "But as I did, he opened his eyes and he thought I was Mamá. He asked if it was all right for him to die. I knew he needed me to say it was. That he could go."

Paul returned her gaze and, as usual, he was burdened. Worried. Yet she knew this time it was worry for her, and even though she was at the mercy of the memory, it strengthened her. And she needed the strength to say the next part.

"I told him he couldn't." Her voice cracked. "I was scared. Jose Luis needed him. I . . . needed him."

She saw Pa's face. The fevered pain in his eyes and the confusion when she told him no, don't die. His chapped lips had mumbled something in Spanish. A phrase she'd never heard before. That's because it wasn't for her. It was for Mamá. All she knew to do was to tell him to calm down. He had become more agitated and he shouted the same phrase again. Then he threw off the quilt and tried to get up. Catalina had struggled to pin him down and he was so ill, she could. He thrashed, fighting against her and the blurry world surrounding him. Jose Luis had stared, his mouth agape in horror.

"Go outside!" Catalina screamed at him as she held Pa down. But Jose Luis didn't listen. He came to the side of the bed, so quietly that she didn't see him at first, and fury sent her spinning when she did. She was trying to protect her brother and he wasn't listening. "Do as I say!"

The shouting only upset Pa more and he flailed beneath her grip. Jose Luis leaned forward and said, "Te amo más que a nada."

Pa quieted. He reached toward Jose Luis and he took his hand. "Josefina?" he croaked. "I hear you."

"Te amo más que a nada," Jose Luis repeated, and Pa's head dropped back on the sweat-drenched pillow.

Catalina breathed hard and sucked in the air. "I just . . . I think those were my last words to him. Telling him not to die."

Paul frowned. It wasn't his usual world-weary frown. It was pensive, quiet. "They don't have to be."

"What?"

"You can still talk to him. Tell him you're . . . sorry or whatever it is you want to say."

Catalina tilted her head back so she could see through the medley of tree branches overhead. The gray sky bent over her. Thoughts of Pa burned in her mind, a nest of vipers made from resentment, anger, confusion.

But maybe, just as she'd misjudged Paul, she'd misjudged Pa too.

"Do you talk your mother?"

Leaning back, Paul looked up at the sky as well. He shook his head. "Naw."

"Why not?"

"Don't know a single thing about her. Anytime I try to reckon who she might be, it feels fake, like I'm telling myself a story to make myself feel better."

Paul's face took on a cynical twist, darkening with so much frustration it seemed to dilute his eyes of color. "I envy you. You're trying to hold on to your memories. I'm trying to forget mine. . . ." He trailed off and lowered his head, as though the weight and pull of the earth were too much to resist.

Catalina's darkest fear was to be alone, family gone, a fear epitomized in the emptiness of the sleep claiming her every night. And it was epitomized by Paul, who walked beside her yet had no one.

Impulsively, she came to a stop. He did too. She leaned against him. Her head came just below his shoulder, and she let her body soften against his. They pressed into each other. With a sharp stab of alarm, Catalina realized that he might feel the coldness from the apple emanating from her pocket. She pulled back.

"The water is close," she said. "Let's get some and then keep going."

She took a step forward and suddenly the ground shifted beneath her. Paul reached out to steady her, but it rolled beneath him too. The entire thin stretch of incline lifted a foot and then came down again. It dropped so quickly that their feet left the earth before they slammed back down into it.

"Harump!" A coarse, low voice came from seemingly beneath them. "Hill Gog! Hill Gog!"

A knob of earth pushed forward and formed into a long, drooping face framed in bushy dirt eyebrows and a bulbous nose. Catalina and Paul beheld the visage that squinted back at them.

"Ruth told us about Hill Gogs too. Remember?" Paul whispered.

"Hill Gog! Hill Gog!" The hill monster crowed in its deep bass voice, as though he'd heard Paul say his name despite him whispering.

"Will you let us pass?" Catalina eyed the creature. She flinched as his jaw fell open, but it was only to yawn. A long and pointed tongue lolled out of his mouth along with a cloud of dust. He sneezed, which sent up more dust, which made him sneeze again.

"Seems friendly," Paul said. "Let's try to slip by." The Hill Gog frowned and grumbled but then his craggy face crinkled into a smile as they walked. He seemed to enjoy their footsteps because he arched back in his hill, shaking like a puppy getting its belly scratched. Once they passed, his eyes closed, and he sank back down into his subterranean home.

The sound of rushing water grew stronger and the thought of easing their parched throats gave them new strength. They pushed through a knob of trees and stopped.

Their path had led them to water, but it was far below. The incline, even steeper at this point, sequestered them away from it. A river, frothy and angry from the heavy winter snows, tumbled along at its base, tantalizingly there but out of reach.

Catalina inched forward to peer down. Whitecaps broke across the water's surface, making it seem as though it boiled. It didn't matter. All she could think was how the water would taste as it crossed her tongue. Then her leg, numb from the apple, buckled. Her body pitched forward and her weight sent her pinwheeling down the ravine. She clawed at the earth, trying to catch hold of anything to stop her from falling into the water.

Roots, scrub, and rocks dug into her, but she couldn't grip them. From afar, she heard the Hill Gog give a low, moaning cry of dismay.

There was a moment of eerie silence. She plummeted into the water.

CHAPTER TWELVE
CATALINA

ICY WATER, SO COLD IT FELT LIKE SHE WAS being stabbed, enveloped Catalina. Giant hands, made entirely from the water, dug through it. They spun the water forward and back, making it a frothy cauldron of rapids. A song, split into different parts, ran across the river. It was much louder when she plunged underneath the surface. It sounded like a work song, and it started to go faster and faster.

The hands churned along to the rhythm of the song, making the water roil and explode across rocks and splash up against the banks. Swift currents closed over her head, drawing her under while simultaneously pushing her forward. Mossy rocks scraped against her body and stripped off her skin in fiery swathes. Catalina kicked, struggling to lift her chin above the surface.

A new song began, and the hands changed their approach. They plunged far down into the river, cupping their hands and creating new, clashing currents. Catalina took a gasping breath of air only to inhale water. It poured down her throat and nose, rushing deep into her lungs. Terror, as merciless and strong as the water, encompassed her. She had to get out. Pa's jacket was a weight dragging her down. She tried to shimmy out of it but she'd buttoned it and it clung heavily on her. Kicking with all her might, she managed to bob up. No matter what, the hands kept digging away, the different pairs working in harmony to turn the river into foamy chaos. Up ahead, she saw a tree slunk half into the water, half out.

It was her only chance. The current pulled her away from it as the work song changed yet again, but she clawed against it. When the river curved and the hands were low beneath the surface, she threw herself at the tree. Its roots hung into the water in a mess of fat helixes. Her fingers reached for the roots, and she managed to grab hold. She twisted herself into them, hair and clothes tangling with the fibrous, meaty strands.

Pulling herself forward, she dragged her body bit by bit from the river. But she couldn't escape. Not fully. Rushing water sucked at her waist and legs and bubbled up to hit her in the face. Her hands clung to the roots, and she willed them to stay closed, to not let go. Darkness blurred her vision and dizziness addled her brain.

"Hill Gog!" she tried to scream. There was no response. She must not lose consciousness. If she did, she would fall back into the water and drown.

There was a grumbling above her. The Hill Gog. He scuttled to the bank, bushy eyebrows drawn together. For a moment, he seemed to consider the situation. Then he dove back down into the dirt. The muddy ground where the earth disintegrated into the riverbed began to spin and spew. Burrowing through the slush, the Hill Gog pushed the dirt into a bank of its own. The heft of the tree lay in the muck and went with it, dragging Catalina along.

She was free. Lying in wet, cold, twig-laden mud but free from the water. Her fingers closed around it, the gritty sludge feeling like silk to her, even as the grime sank beneath her nails.

"Thank you," she croaked but the Hill Gog was already scampering away. Then, she heard her name shouted in Paul's voice. It drew closer and closer and then he was above her, a hazy shape rimmed in light. He bent over and hoisted her into his arms. Cold set in and she started shaking, teeth chattering so hard she felt like they might break against each other. There was no strength in her body but she turned her face into his shoulder, inhaling the solidity and strength of him. He carried her away from the muddy bank and set her down on dry ground.

"You're soaked," he said, panic lurking just underneath his firm voice. "We need to get you dry."

Catalina's fingers were thick with numbness and achy with chill. She struggled to shed the layers of her sodden clothes. Paul peeled off his shirt. The jacket and jorongo fell from her into a sopping pile, but she couldn't undo the buttons of her blouse. Paul undid them for her, forcing the buttons through their holes with desperate motions. She shucked it and he wrapped his shirt around her and, as quickly as he had undone the buttons on her blouse, fastened the buttons up the front of the shirt. Her hands went to the waistband of her skirt but she could barely get them to open or close. Paul glanced at her questioningly and she nodded. His hands reached up under the shirt, brushing the undersides of her ribs and across her stomach as he undid the clasps. The skirt and petticoat slopped to the ground. Steadying her, he helped her step free of them, her bare legs bristling. She sank down and, weakly, she pulled her knees up into the shirt. It was large enough but thin, the flannel nothing against the fierce cold sweeping through her bloodstream and settling in her bones.

"Here." Paul moved behind her and pulled her back into him, draping his arms around her. She leaned into his warmth, seeking it to save her from the bitter chill. Fearful realizations tumbled over her in an unrelenting chain. Her clothes were soaked. They had nothing to make a fire, no food, no blankets. Once night came, they would be at its brutal mercy. Already, the sky was stained with the purple and blue splotches of twilight.

"Night is coming," she said, teeth chattering so much that it was hard to force the words out. "What will we do?"

"Stay like this," Paul said grimly against her ear, his voice the only warmth she felt. "It's our only choice."

They knew what the cold was like at night. They'd already spent two days outside. But nothing could've prepared Catalina for how it felt with no fire, blankets, or proper clothes.

From deep in the woods, wails of tree weepers floated to them. Their sobbing seemed to intensify as the night went on until it almost became howls. Other new, strange things roused. In the highest branches of the trees, winged, glowing creatures with pointed teeth and tiny horns fluttered like bats. They chattered to each other in whiney huffs but didn't seem to notice Catalina and Paul far below. Sometimes they fought and other times they seemed to dance together, jittering through the sky.

Paul started to shiver but Catalina was frozen past shivering. Only her lips quivered. She curled into him, face pressed against his naked chest. His arms clasped around her, and his legs were drawn up, as though his body was a shelter to save her. Sleep was impossible for her but, at some point, Paul drowsed off. She listened to him mumble, his head twisting back and forth. There was a new word in his nightmares tonight. *Catalina.*

Toward early dawn, she wondered if they might die there, or at the very least, if she might—White Spider tree vision be damned. Her hair stiffened into frosty ropes around her face and formed icicles down her back. Mud gritted between her teeth. Her limbs were absent yet livid things, half deadened into numbness, half needled through with pinpricks of cold. Mind drifting, she thought about how the bride had told Paul that once you set aside your body, you realized how hot and itchy it was. Hers wasn't hot and itchy, but it felt like something she was wearing, something heavy and wooden that wouldn't mind at all to stay here forever, pressed against the earth.

"Catalina?" Paul stirred beneath her, trembling without his shirt. "Are you there?"

"Must be," she croaked. *Must be.* She repeated the two words over and over in her mind like they were a poem she was trying to memorize, until the sun began to rise. Darkness receded but, as it did, it wove a frigid morning mist over them like a death spell. Finally, gold rays glimmered through the mist and, after a long while, Catalina felt its warmth. The winged creatures settled, roosting for the day, and the tree weepers' howls softened into sobbing.

Slowly, she sat forward in the tangle of Paul's arms and twisted to look at him. His eyelids and lips were often stained with purple, but now they were almost black.

"Paul?" she said hoarsely. "Paul!"

He stirred, frowning as though hearing her from far away. His lashes fluttered, struggling to open, and he squinted at her.

"Good morning," he said with effort.

"We should move around. Get warm."

"You do that," he mumbled. "I'll . . . be right there."

Drawing in a breath for strength, she rose. Then she looked down. She'd forgotten she only wore his shirt. It came to just above her knees. She'd never been in such a state of undress around a boy before and the realization sent a peculiar warmth through her, one not from the sun. Somehow, it didn't bother her to be this way in front of Paul, a thought even more alarming than the first. She reached for her clothes. Still wet. She slipped into the petticoat. It was the thinnest garment, so it was the driest, but it sent cloying damp against her skin. She realized, with horror, that only one of her shoes was there. The other must have been lost in the river.

Sinking down, the bleakness of the situation spread out before her like a picnic of misfortunes. She was battered from the river and her head still throbbed from the bride striking her. Paul didn't seem well at all. Not only did they not have food, matches for a fire, or blankets, but she was missing a shoe. And, most terrifyingly, Don Pedro was still gone. They could keep heading in the direction he'd been flying but . . . then what? For how long? What

if he'd meant to turn at a certain point? They would never know
and just keep pushing on into the wilderness.

The apple. Quickly, she reached for Pa's jacket. Somehow, it
was there.

"What are you looking for?" Glancing over her shoulder, she
saw Paul watching her through half-closed eyes.

"Nothing. We should get going. But you need your shirt."

"Keep it," Paul mumbled. "You need it more than I do.
Everything else is still wet."

"Are you certain?"

"Unless I'm too much of a distraction without it. . . ."
Somehow, his joke drew her eyes to his torso. The cold night
and the havoc wreaked by the cholera seemed to have shrunk
his skin against his muscles. He looked more marble than
mortal, a statue hewn in deathly strokes of blueish gray. The
sight harrowed her.

If he just moved around, he could warm up and shake off
the pallor. She thought about wrapping him in the jorongo
and Pa's jacket, but the jorongo was still wet and she worried it
would make him worse. The jacket, as thick as it was, was even
wetter than the jorongo, and she couldn't risk him finding the
apple. Biting her lip, she slipped them on, shivering as the damp
fabric settled against her skin. They were still wet, but Paul's
shirt helped protect her. They would have to dry as they walked.
Determined to get them going again and get Paul's blood circu-
lating, she turned to him.

"Here, let me help you up." She tried to help him to his feet.
He struggled upward and managed to stand. Then his knees
buckled, and he slumped to the ground.

"Damn it," he muttered under his breath. Gently, Catalina touched his forehead. It was clammy and cold, but a fever ran hot through him.

"Rest," she murmured.

"Don't want to."

"You need to. It was cold last night."

"No, we need to keep going."

"Now you sound like me," she said with a slight smile.

"I just . . . I don't want to die here." The plaintive note in his voice stole Catalina's breath. She fought off a shudder and leaned toward him.

"Certainly not. You only need a little rest." But her words were hollow to even her. Something was wrong with him. Of course, something had always been wrong. She could tell the cholera had been cruel. Now, though, the odd sheen of sweat pasted his hair to his forehead as though he'd been drenched in the river, not her. His breath had a wheezing whine to it too. This whole time, he'd seemed one step ahead of the ailment. But now it seemed to have caught him. The thought made Catalina's stomach turn and she abruptly pulled back, turning away as though that alone could block out the reality.

"I know you have an apple," he said suddenly.

Startled, Catalina stared at him, one hand instinctively covering the pocket where it rested. There was no point in denying it. She said, "I thought maybe I would take a bite. John would come and I could slash his seed bag. It might end his curse, and he'd have no power over Jose Luis. And I think I should. It's our only option."

"It won't work. You'll die."

"We don't know that for sure. What if I just take a tiny bite? It might be all right."

"Won't matter. I know it for a fact."

"But how?"

"I—I need to tell you something," Paul said. A new dread thickened in Catalina's throat, making it hard to swallow. She sank down next to him. "You know how I said I was hired by a town? There was a reason I was. I was there because I'd been traveling with my logging crew. We'd been on the move for several days when we came across a wild apple orchard." Haltingly, he struggled. "We were coming from a remote logging camp in New York. Most of the men hadn't been to town in months, but I'd gone to get us some supplies before we headed up to the Wisconsin River. When I did, I heard rumors about apple trees that killed you. I laughed. You know how information gets twisted as it travels around. When we stumbled onto the orchard, I almost spoke up. Suggested we go around."

The dread in Catalina's throat intensified, so much so she felt as though she couldn't even breathe.

"But I was afraid. Afraid of looking stupid . . . to the men, because it would mean my father was right about me." A wince crossed his face, and he started speaking faster, as though wanting it out at once. "So, I didn't say anything and, as we walked into the orchard, it began. The apples whispered to us. I took one and I knew I was holding my own death, but the pull was so strong. Too strong."

He shuddered and she almost told him to stop, to rest. But the story entangled her, left her at its mercy, only able to listen.

"I took a bite. We all did. The birds sang. It took a bit longer for me to be affected but then I collapsed, and I saw him. The Man of Sap. Standing over me and seeming . . . confused. For a long time, he paced back and forth. Finally, everything went black, and I thought I'd died. I woke up in the town. They told me I was out for a whole week and that all my friends had been killed by the apples. It was the last good sleep I ever got. Since then, I've had nightmares. I know the apple's killing me, just slower than most. So I decided since I'm basically a draining hourglass, I might as well stop the bastard behind it. Avenge my friends. They really were the only family I've ever known. And maybe it's more than that. Maybe I want to do something, be something, before I die, instead of just what my father says."

Catalina realized why he'd said he didn't need to touch the White Spider tree. He already knew what waited for him. She didn't know what to say but leaned her head against his shoulder. He wrapped his arm around her, pulling her into him. Almost desperately, she buried her face into his chest, and they clung to each other as though the other might save them.

With her face pressed against him, she heard his heart. It beat out a metrical tempo and she listened until it skipped a beat. Or maybe she imagined it, because she was terrified of it skipping, tripping, stopping. She pushed back from him, back from the body that was betraying him, and captured his face in her hands. He caught his breath and held it so he was still, completely still, and Catalina longed to pull in close again.

No secrets remained between them. If she just closed those few inches, no distance would remain either. She could press her lips to his and inhale everything that was him. Drag her hands through his hair and trace the lines of his neck with her fingers. But while he held his breath, hers wrenched in her throat through the aching lump of dread and turned into a broken sob. Roughly, she pushed his face away from her, as she had his body, and rose to her feet.

Sor Juana wrote a poem called "Love Opened a Mortal Wound" and it flashed through Catalina's mind, even though she forbad it.

Love opened a mortal wound.
In agony, I worked the blade
to make it deeper.

Paul was one more face to add to her three. A face to lose, a soul to be claimed while hers stayed behind. She couldn't do it. She couldn't add a fourth. Because while John's curse set her on this path, she bore the worst one of all: to be alive and powerless, unable to hold her loved ones to this place. The more she loved, the deeper she worked the blade.

"Catalina?" Paul said her name, voice thick with hurt.

"I can't."

"Can't what?"

"Everyone I love has died or is in danger of dying," she said. Saying it aloud took her back to Pa's grave, where she'd stood with an unfinished poem in her heart and her father buried at her feet. Dirt waited to receive all who she loved, all that she loved. "I can't be anything to you, Paul, and you can't be anything to me."

"But aren't we already? You mean something to me, Catalina. I'm not afraid to say it, even if I die at the end of this. I've faced death before. In the logging accident where I got my scar and then again after eating the apple. I didn't want to die those times, sure. But more because I was a wound clock, already running and set to go, to be. But with you, it isn't that I don't want to die. I want to live. It's because, for the first time ever, there is someone who gives a damn . . . or so I thought . . . and who can say what will happen? Maybe if John's curse ends, things will be made right. We don't know. We don't know anything, it seems, and there's room in mysteries, Catalina, room for things to be different. For them to be all right."

"No." Catalina answered with such passion it could be mistaken for anger. "Stop it. Don't you see? Nothing can be made right. I've seen it over and over again. There are no mysteries in which things can be made different, just graves. I'm not able to save the people I love, Paul."

At that, Catalina's passion did become anger. Anger at the circumstances that put her with this dying boy while she tried to rescue her brother. Why hadn't he told her? Why did he run into the burning barn for her books and hold her all night against the cold and stare at her in a way she'd never been stared at before?

Her hand closed around the apple. She pulled it out of her pocket. The bright red orb shone in her hand. She didn't know if it was a beacon to light her way or a flame that would consume her. But she did know she would do anything to save the ones she loved.

"What are you doing?" Panic laced Paul's voice. "Give it to me, Catalina."

Swiftly, she drew it to her lips. With the last of his strength, Paul lunged forward, trying to knock it away.

He was too late.

Catalina took a bite.

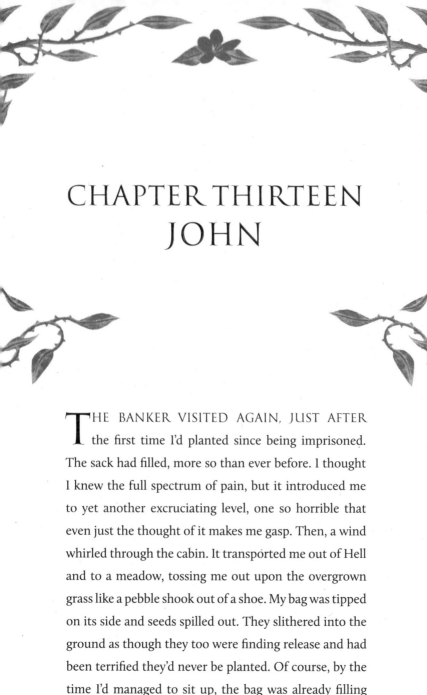

CHAPTER THIRTEEN
JOHN

THE BANKER VISITED AGAIN, JUST AFTER the first time I'd planted since being imprisoned. The sack had filled, more so than ever before. I thought I knew the full spectrum of pain, but it introduced me to yet another excruciating level, one so horrible that even just the thought of it makes me gasp. Then, a wind whirled through the cabin. It transported me out of Hell and to a meadow, tossing me out upon the overgrown grass like a pebble shook out of a shoe. My bag was tipped on its side and seeds spilled out. They slithered into the ground as though they too were finding release and had been terrified they'd never be planted. Of course, by the time I'd managed to sit up, the bag was already filling again.

"You did well," the banker said, opening the cupboard and rummaging around. "Where are the teacups?" He spotted them, smashed to delicate smithereens of floral print and dusty rose porcelain against the wall. "Oh. Now what shall we use for our coffee?"

Staring down at my bark-covered hands, I didn't answer. All I could think about was the meadow and how it was my fault it was sown through with death. Just like all the places I'd planted before. Just like all the places yet to come.

"Why are you here?" I asked desolately.

"We are both men on the fringes, John. There are others like you, but most hate me so much, it's impossible to have, well, a cup of coffee. Certainly, you aren't fond of me. But you hate yourself most of all. Though it wasn't very hospitable of you to destroy the teacups. Those were from the royal collection of the Habsburgs."

I shrugged sullenly. The seed bag was lighter since I'd just planted but it was filling steadily. Soon, I would have to plant again. My contract bound me, soul and body. I thought back to the paper I'd signed. It'd happened long ago. Vaguely, I remembered my name at the top and so many tiny, fancy words underneath it. So many, many words.

I sat upright.

"I want to see my contract."

The banker frowned. He reached into the cupboard, found a tin cup, and sighed. "Whatever for?"

"I have the right to see it."

"That is true. Every man has a right to his own contract." He reached inside his jacket and withdrew the papers. Just as I remembered, my name was inscribed across the top in fancy calligraphy. I snatched it from him. "Is there something specifically you're looking for?"

"A way out."

"No one finds a way out." The banker's voice was flat, unemotional. "You might as well give it up."

I almost did. I was so used to defeat it was hard to even conceive of anything else. Then I came to a clause: *The banker shall possess John Chapman's soul until he empties the seed sack.*

Impulsively, I set the contract aside and surged to my feet. I brushed by the banker and grabbed a knife. Stabbing it into the bag, I drew a long slit in its side. Seeds drained. Forbidden hope sparked. But then the frayed, grainy edges of burlap stretched toward each other. Thin threads strung across the slit like a weaver spider spinning its silks. The threads pulled tight in a single moment. The slit was gone. The sack had mended itself.

"Creative," the banker said, going to set the kettle over the fire. "But you cannot free yourself, Johnny."

I looked from the knife I still held and then back at the bag. "Could someone else free me?"

"Persistent, aren't you? I suppose your seeds could free you, if they stopped filling the bag. But they do not wish to. They wish to be planted. They always will. They seek life in the way a flower explodes with pollen to seek new soil as it dies. Like any other thing in nature, they wish to live."

Thinking hard, I set the knife down and absentmindedly picked at the bark on the back of my hand. Marguerite's red hair ribbon, now drained into a limp, colorless strip, swung from my wrist. Closing my eyes, I imagined her lying across the hotel bed during our honeymoon, long before I'd destroyed our lives. I could see her bright smile and hear her saying, "You are clever and formidable. Don't let anyone tell you otherwise, mon cheri."

My spirit had long been broken but her words came to me like a message from an angel. What if there was a way around the banker's contract? I thought about what he said. My seeds could free me. Seeds. An idea came to me and with it, a plan. I stood just as the kettle sang. Its whistle sang along with a new, cautious idea in my head.

Removing it from the fire, I smiled at the banker.

"Let's get you that coffee."

❀

CATALINA

Crisp skin gave way to soft, sweet flesh.

Never had Catalina realized such flavors existed. The apple tasted like a fine red wine, its notes coming in rich volleys of honeyed sweetness and tart earthiness. It was exquisitely poignant on her tongue. Even as she ate, she starved for more. Juice dripped down her hands and chin. She lifted the apple to take another bite. All the world seemed contained in the apple and she wanted to consume it, swallow it, become it.

"Stop! No!" Paul grabbed it from her and flung it down the hillside. "Catalina!"

He said her name in the way Pa called out Mamá's name at night, waking from sleep to remember she was dead. But Catalina was possessed. She wanted more. She needed more. She pushed him aside, ready to fling herself down the drop-off just to get one more bite.

Then it felt like she was being torn apart. Fire gutted her throat, tracing the way the apple had gone down. Every bit of her skin enflamed, and her eyes burned as a sticky substance filled them like tears.

As it did, it happened. Just as Pa had always said.

All of it—the high and low punctuations of birdcalls, the fingers of the wind up in the trees, the rattling hum of cicadas in the bushes—fell away. Silence, the sort that you never find in the wilderness, cupped itself over the woods. Catalina heard a single bird. It let out a long note and it swelled into a song, as melodious as a mournful fiddle. The tune seemed to whisper over her. It was full of sadness, made sweeter by its darkness. More birds joined it, the same as Don Pedro. They appeared on branches, hanging on them like crimson flowers, singing as one. Wind grew, whipped around her, and blew her skirt up past her knees.

As quickly as it came, the wind died. She knew, then.

The Man of Sap was here.

She'd only seen John once. The image was striking, framed in vibrant hues of fear. He creaked toward her, the sound like a low hiss that she didn't seem to hear but felt, slithering up her spine to her neck. The creaking drew close, and the scent of old wood and old sweat stung her nose. With the sun at his back, John was more tree than ever. He stood over her and his form crumpled as he fell to his knees. Leaves spiraled from his hair and brushed gently across her cheeks. He plunged his face into his hands. A high-pitched moan came from him.

Catalina vaguely thought that she was going somewhere, but how could that be? Still, she swore she heard Mamá's singing. It was soft, a murmur riding the breeze to reach her. Catalina hadn't heard it for years and she groped for it, as though she could catch it and close her hands around it and hold it forever. She wasn't in pain any longer. The realization was startling. It wasn't simply that her head didn't hurt or that she wasn't cold. It was that the erosion of her soul, the one that had begun years ago when Mamá died on a sunny day and Catalina realized the world held a blade and waited to bleed her dry, was gone. As though it had never been, as though something had been unbroken in her, as though she'd been set free.

Then she heard Paul, far away and muffled, and saw John, staring down at her. *Jose Luis*. She'd forgotten as she lay dying.

She couldn't go.

Not now.

Weak and limp, her hand went to Pa's knife and she struggled to unsheathe it. To her surprise, John didn't pull back. His mouth formed words she couldn't hear. The air around him rippled, just as it had when he'd taken her brother. He was leaving, a part of him was pulling away from this reality and into another. The shoulder with the bag disappeared. All Catalina had time to do was let go of the knife handle so it fell back into its sheath and grab his hand and fumble her other one out for Paul. He reached back for it. Everything fractured into a thousand pieces.

In an immediate mad rush, she was falling. But it didn't seem to be down or up. It was the motion without the direction, wind gusting over her and tumbling her about. John's rough hand and Paul's desperate fingers tore away, and she was alone. Her limbs flailed, trying to find something to grab ahold of in the emptiness. But there was nothing to grasp in the pockets between places. This was the way John traveled. She was merely subject to the journey, a passenger whirling toward an unknown destination.

Then, she was abruptly released and she found herself lying on her back, gasping. Her body tingled from the onslaught of the wind, and it felt as though a hundred flashing lights blinked on and off beneath her skull.

Blurriness fogged everything into dim, skittering shapes. She struggled to bring her hand to her face to wipe away the tears streaming from her eyes. Bit by bit, the hazy world sharpened into focus. Still gulping air, she looked around.

For a second, she thought bars surrounded her. But that wasn't right. She wasn't caged in by bars, but by trees. They grew side by side in an arrangement too orderly for nature. Branches spread out in forked claws. Oozing red sap collected like pools of blood around each one. Bark formed cavernous ridges and there were *things* embedded within them. Catalina squinted and then let out a harsh breath. Bones and teeth, both gleaming white in the dim light, filled the grooves—along with apples. It was as though the trunks were macabre curio cabinets, the bark forming long shelves and tiny boxes to showcase their grisly collection.

Catalina pulled back and looked up. An angry red firmament hung suffocatingly close. It didn't seem to be the sky, but the underside of the ground. Roots, stringy and gnarled, poked through it, and hung lifelessly above her head. When she raised her hand, the roots and firmament receded. Sinister sounds slunk around her, distinguishing themselves into their own chords, which they repeated over and over. The barking cough of foxes, the dry rustle of snakes through brush, and the regurgitating gag of owls. Flashes immersed the world in a baptism of white light every few minutes, followed by a retort of thunder. But it heralded no rain, and heat breathed a hot and heavy breath over her, painting sweat across Catalina's back and the nape of her neck. She should take off the jacket and jorongo. They were sweltering her. But she couldn't. Wouldn't. Somewhere along the way, the two items had become her armor, her shield, her shelter.

A figure limped toward her through the trees.

"Paul!"

"Catalina?" He stopped right before they reached each other. "Where are we?"

"I think . . ." Swallowing hard, she looked around. "Not anywhere good."

"Insightful," Paul said dryly, his gaze flickering nervously around. Then it settled on her face, a confliction of relief and grief. "You are all right?"

"I am." The heaviness of her heart and the weight of her losses was back, but all the physical pain she'd felt after biting the apple was gone. Nothing burned in her eyes or throat. The realization was like a splinter slipping into her skin, an uneasiness that lingered under her thoughts. Why was she better? "You look terrible."

He did. The wheezing sound still hitched in his breath, and the glow of fever burned even brighter in his eyes. There was no need for a shirt since it was so warm here but without it, she saw just how much his shoulders hunched. His every move was sluggish, pained, as though he was slowly trudging into a nightmare from which he wouldn't awaken. Gently, she put a hand to his forehead. Almost against her will, her hand curved down to his cheek. She pulled it away.

"John must be here, somewhere," she said, refusing to look at Paul. "Jose Luis must be too." The thought of her brother trapped in this place made her want to retch. Jose Luis was a boy of the woods, his heart always singing its own birdcall. This place had trees, but it almost made it worse. It was a wilderness drained of life and hope. She'd only just arrived and wanted out. *Needed* out. "Maybe I can climb one of the trees and see further."

"Be careful," Paul said. "They don't look very nice."

They certainly didn't. As she approached the closest one, it clicked and gurgled, the unusual sounds edged with threat. Tentatively, she put her hand on it. Sticky red sap oozed over her fingers, but she was able to grab hold of a low branch and pull herself onto it. She moved from branch to branch, higher and higher, the tree shifting beneath her as its clicks grew louder. Pa's jacket and the jorongo were much too hot to wear here but as she climbed, she was grateful for their protection against the rough bark. The bones, teeth, and apples embedded in their clefts trembled and knocked against each other in a disconcerting clatter. Finally, she climbed high enough to see beyond the other trees. Clutching the trunk, she turned outward.

The sight sent her heart plummeting. Trees spread in every direction. There seemed to be no actual intersection between them and the red sky. They simply continued, horizonless and parallel to each other. Every few minutes, a jagged spear of white lightning tore the empty space between them, preceding the low, rumbling thunder. Horror claimed her, followed by a dread so thick and heavy she nearly lost her grip.

Then she gasped. A narrow column of smoke rose from one of the trees, the sort from a fireplace. Never had she been so grateful. It meant there was something out there in the vast nothingness. And that was the place they should go.

Quickly, she climbed back down. Paul waited, slumped against one of the trees.

"I think I saw where John's home is," she said. "It doesn't seem too far. We just need to walk straight, and we'll come upon it. Can you manage?"

"Don't really have a choice." Mouth set grimly, Paul struggled upright. "I'll be damned if I lay down and die here. It's too . . . red."

"It is very red." Catalina was amused despite herself. She slipped her arm around his waist, but he stepped away.

"Maybe you should go on ahead. I don't want to slow you down. I can rest and catch up. At this point, I'm likely more of a liability than anything else."

"I'm not leaving you here."

"It's all right. Maybe it'd make it easier."

"Make what easier?" she demanded.

He hesitated. "I don't know. Dying. Or not having to be near you."

"I can't be that abhorrent," she said, gently teasing.

"Abhorrent? Catalina, I want to pull you in my arms and kiss you properly. I want to make every wrong in the world right so you won't ever hurt again. I want to build you a house and fill it with books. I want to—" He stopped, turning away as though she were the sun and unwise to stare.

Catalina's hands seemed to move of their own accord. They reached for his face, caught it, held it, and she realized the last time this had happened, she'd pushed him away.

Now there was no pushing away and her hands found their way to his chest. She felt the way she had for the past nights, staring up at the sky. That she was at the mercy of an immense unknown and if she stepped into it—if she kissed him—she would never find her way back. But she'd realized something else. Learned something from the regret that shadowed her from earlier.

If she didn't kiss him and she lost him, her regret would be far worse.

CHAPTER FOURTEEN
JOHN

THIS NEXT PART IS HARD. MAYBE THE HARDEST of everything that's happened to me, which I'm sure is shocking considering the horrors I've both dealt and endured. The bag filled quickly, and the wind came to take me to plant. This time, though, I had a plan.

The banker had said the seeds could free me. Well, there were more seeds in the world than just the sort you plant. Children were seeds of their parents. So perhaps my son could slash the bag and stop it from filling?

Once the wind deposited me in the woods north of Wisconsin, I didn't dump out the bag as usual. Instead, I reached into it. It was hideously difficult. The pain, built up as the bag filled back in Hell, was intolerable. I only took a few handfuls. As the seeds found the ground, the agony eased until it was manageable. As long as I was actively planting, I could walk about the world as I wished, and the wind did not come for me. It bought me time.

As I dropped my seeds, I searched for my son, avoiding humans. It was a difficult task. Time passed differently in Hell than it did on earth. Years seemed to jump on earth, all of vitality rushing into the future, while time in Hell sat behind in a yawning vacuum. I did not like traveling about in this way. Instead of sowing seeds in open areas, I was dropping them along roads and towns, which meant eventually they would be filled with my evil trees. Instead of being concentrated in one area, they would be everywhere. But it was my only choice.

First, I found Marguerite.

It turned out that she'd passed some years ago and had been buried next to her parents, her gravestone inscribed in her native French. My little sun had died. At midnight, I stood before her grave, holding vigil until dawn, clutching seeds in my hand but refusing to plant them. There would be no making things right between us ever again. When dawn flushed the sky with yellow, I slipped away, leaving an apple atop her gravestone. Not one of mine. Just an apple, as I'd always promised her.

After I'd found her grave, I eventually located my son living in Michigan Territory. He was married, with children, my grand-children. They lived in a settlement, but far down an empty road as though they didn't belong with the bustle of everyone else. Everything about their lives was small. The cabin was tiny, the chickens few, the garden only a few yards wide. Even they them-selves seemed tiny against the largeness of the world. But it was a good kind of small. Tight. Protected. Stronger for its intimacy.

There were four of them and they formed one happy heart, each seeming to receive and give light from the others. A wife, a boy, a girl, and my son.

I gathered my courage. My son would know his father was a monster. I knew what that was like and disgrace almost made me retreat. But he might be the only one who could save me. Once he understood the stakes, I had no doubt he would slit the bag. Even if he hated me, he would do it to save everyone else from my evil bounties.

On a warm and sunny day, I went to the cabin and observed it from behind a tree. My plan was to approach my son alone. There was no need to scare the children. I wondered what he would say. What he would think.

I was busy watching when a voice demanded, "Who are you?" I turned around. The wife stood there, hair pinned into a sleek bun. "*What* are you?"

"I'm . . ." I didn't know what to say. I hadn't spoken with a person who wasn't dying at my feet in a long time. "I'm John."

"¡Dios mío!" Stepping back, her face hollowed with fear. Her hand fluttered in the sign of a cross.

"I don't mean any harm." I wanted to explain things to her. Maybe if I did, she wouldn't be scared. Maybe she would help me talk to my son, her husband. "I'm just like you. Or I used to be but now I plant apple trees and they are, well, cursed." One of my birds, sitting atop my pot hat, cawed at her. She cringed. "Your husband, Gabriel . . . is he near? I've been looking for him."

That's when I heard a growl and a crashing through the woods. Looking over my shoulder, I gasped. A hulking creature lumbered toward us. I thought it was a bear, but then I saw glowing red eyes set far back in the dark mass of a furry head. I knew. This was not a bear at all. Strings of saliva dripped from jagged teeth and bony hooks ringed the snout. I planted myself between it and the woman, but the ground reverberated with its strength. There was no way I could stop it. The woman took a few steps back but didn't flee.

"Get away!"

The animal roared, its pointed teeth as red and glowing as its eyes. Why wasn't she running? Then I realized she was blocking a path, one that led to the cabin. She didn't want to lead the animal toward it. She was trying to protect something. The last thing I saw before the animal barreled over was her eyes—full of fear yet also full of purpose.

I imagined being hit by the solid weight of the animal was similar to being hit by one of those newfangled steam engines. If I were mortal, I would've been dead on impact. But I wasn't. Instead, I spun through the air, bones snapping like twigs. Even before they reknit, I jumped to my feet through will alone. I threw myself at the animal as it mauled the woman and tried to tear it away with my bare hands. I snapped off my own wrist to form a sharp point of bone and wood and impaled it. But it didn't matter. Once it was over, the animal lumbered off, leaving me alone with the woman. Wheezing gasps rent the air and I knew what it was—or should I say, what it meant. I was long accustomed to death and its sounds. Dragging myself to her, I saw thick rivulets of blood leaking from a wound on her chest. My own wrist was hemorrhaging sap, but I didn't care. With my good hand, I tried to stem the bleeding.

From afar, I heard a shout. I scrambled away and ducked behind a tree, just as a thin man with spectacles ran to the woman. Gabriel.

"Josefina! My God!" He fell to his knees beside her, pulling her into his lap. "Help!"

She grabbed his wrist, shaking her head. "Don't let them see," she choked. "Don't let the children see."

"It'll be all right. You'll be all right!" His body shook as though he was sobbing, but no tears fell. They stared into each other's eyes, his face twisted in horror and hers twisted in grief.

"It was a man . . . a man of sap . . . protect the children. He . . . he's looking for you . . . don't let him get the children. He plants apple trees. Cursed apple trees."

"Shhhh, don't talk." He cradled her to his chest and her blood stained his clothes. "Stay still."

"I love you," she said and then she whispered something in Spanish. I was familiar with the language from my travels, but not enough to understand what she was saying. Gabriel answered.

I fled, all the way back to Hell. There, I tried to wash my hands but no matter what I did, the blood remained. It had soaked deep into the ridges of my bark. Stains, as dark on the outside as they were on the inside. I'd killed Gabriel's wife—or I'd gotten her killed. I'd led the banker right to her. It was all my fault.

Please know that a day doesn't go by when I don't think about her. I replay her death in my mind so often, it seems as though I can enter the lost moment and fix it, do it differently. But it will always be as it was. Just as the banker's poor creations will always exist, even as time erodes them to dust, they will *be*.

So I repeat the things she said in my head. They were ordinary, as far as the things people say when unexpectedly dying. No one is ready for their last words, after all. She spoke of her children. She told my son she loved him.

Ordinary words, perhaps. Yet the sort that defy every ordinary thing.

CATALINA

Their lips met, cautiously. But while the kiss was gentle, Catalina clutched Paul, her nails digging into him. He pulled her against him, weak yet driven. She undid the button of Pa's jacket and slid it off with the jorongo. Both his hands reached beneath the flannel shirt and wrapped around her waist to run down the sloping arch of her back and settle near the waistband of her petticoat. There was finesse to the motion. He made her feel like a porcelain teacup, one that had been set much too close to the edge of a table, one about to fall and shatter on the floor. Only, strangely, she wanted to shatter.

Somewhere, thunder, an ominous brontide, rumbled. In the far reaches of Catalina's mind, she knew that wasn't right. Lightning came first, not thunder. This time, though, it was reversed. The lightning exploded above them, dousing them in white light. Likely she'd just gotten confused, but never had she been so alive and so aware, and yet so hopelessly lost to the boy before her.

She didn't know if she exhaled or inhaled, but a sound of breathless abandon came from her. He stopped. Only not really. Every bit of him shook and she didn't know if it was from fever or desire.

He forced out between clenched teeth, "Did I hurt you?"

"Yes," she panted. His grip was painfully strong, even though he didn't mean for it to be. "Don't stop."

Their lips met again, and he grasped her hips, lifting her up so everything was only him, only his hands, only his arms, only his gaze burning into hers. Then he staggered, woozy and off-balance. His movements became slow and sloppy. His eyes glittered with frustrated desperation. Gently, she stopped him and held his face in her hands again and then eased his head against her shoulder. Every breath was labored, dragging in and out of his body with effort. They sank down to the ground to sit. Leaning against him, Catalina—despite where they were and why and what might come—was happy. She realized, then, the nice thing about being lost.

You could be found.

When Paul was strong enough, they continued toward John's home. Catalina put on Pa's jacket and the jorongo again and her heart pounded, beating in tempo with the thoughts in her head. Paul was dying. She had kissed him, opening a new mortal wound and digging the blade deeper by her own hand. Everything unsaid between them had somehow been said as his mouth found its way down her neck, like ink dried to paper in words forever bound to it. There was no regret, but she thought of the bride haunting New Appleton, and swore she could smell dead wedding flowers.

It was a relief when smoke filled her nose, overpowering the phantom reek of dried roses. Up ahead, a clearing pushed back the trees to form an opening in the woods. They slowed.

"John must be here . . . and Jose Luis," Catalina said, breathless. "Look, there's seeds . . . and a cabin."

It was true. Wood channels cut through the clearing and seeds flowed through them like water. The channels directed the seeds out of the clearing and into the woods, where they seemed to continue. The seeds poured through cracks in the cabin.

For its part, the cabin was perched like a delicate birdhouse in the arms of an apple tree. Its trunk grew through the cabin's center, exploding through its shingled roof in a dense canopy of leaves, branches, and apples, and holding it far off the ground. Stairs notched their way up the trunk to a red door. The smoke that Catalina had seen streamed from a silvery vent in the wood, and yellow light gleamed out from behind two windows, framed in actual glass, not greased paper. Gently, the cabin rocked back and forth. The motion made two sets of shutters wink open and closed and the door croak on rusty hinges. The tree's branches agitatedly moved around it, the apples shivering from their stems. Every now and then, one of its branches brushed the ground and rested for a moment, only to spring up again.

John's birds sat on the trees surrounding the clearing. Their eyes were closed, and their wings folded against their bodies. Don Pedro didn't seem to be among them. Maybe her old bird companion had never found his way back.

Catalina unsheathed Pa's knife and Paul, weak as he was, undid his ax.

"Up the stairs?" she whispered. "If John is in there, we can catch him unawares. I can slit his bag. But we need to move fast and quietly."

"All right." A muscle flexed in Paul's jaw, a subtle display of resilience despite his state. "Let's go."

Silent as shadows, they moved into the clearing. They crouched low and stayed close to the runnels. Catalina's head pounded in pain and fear. Branches of the apple tree swooped over their heads, cutting through the air like the undersides of ship hulls. By the time they reached the stairs, Paul was gasping. But there was no time to stop. They stayed to one side of the stairs and ascended. Paul struggled to catch his breath with each step. It seemed to skip ahead of him, never his to fully grasp.

They reached the door and stopped right outside it. Catalina tried to look inside the narrow slit between the door and its frame. Someone was crouched against the trunk in the center of the space. A boy with messy hair. Catalina thought she was imagining her brother. She blinked, certain he'd disappear. But he didn't. He was there.

Taking a ragged breath, she nodded at Paul.

They charged into the cabin with their weapons aloft.

"Catalina?" Jose Luis cried.

She spun in a circle, balancing against the listing cabin. John was nowhere to be seen.

In three steps, she crossed the floor to Jose Luis, dropped Pa's knife, and pulled him close, as close as humanly possible. His frame, in all its knobby familiarity, pressed against her. The irrational thought flared that she would never let him go. That her arms would be enough to protect him from any harm to come, if she just held on tight enough.

"I knew you'd come," Jose Luis said. It was as though they were young again, in the woods, where sacred magic encircled them.

"Are you all right?" She pulled back to search his face. It was haggard. Pinpoints of firelight bounced off new hollows, as though he was more ghoul than boy. "What happened to your arm?"

White cloth wrapped around his forearm. Gingerly, he unwound it. The cloth fell away, revealing an angry redness covering it from wrist to elbow. Catalina grabbed his hand and stared. Her stomach twisted. Blisters rose in the red patches, popped, and rose again, like bubbles in a boiling pot of water.

"It's from cider," Jose Luis said. "He made me drink it and it's been getting worse."

"Don't worry." She spoke fast, but it was happening. Evil had reached into their sacred circle. No matter how many lines she drew, it always found its way to them. She glanced around. The cabin was small. There was the fireplace carved out of the trunk, a cracked mirror, a table, two armchairs, and a bed covered in a red and blue quilt. Seeds poured from a door off to one side. They ran along the sides of the cabin and out its cracks, where the runnels caught and directed them. "I'll find a way to make it better. John will pay for what he's done."

"It wasn't John," Jose Luis said. "It was someone else. He calls himself the banker. Catalina, he says the cider is going to kill me."

The banker. The bride had mentioned him. Catalina looked over Jose Luis's head to meet Paul's eyes. Paul returned her gaze with grimness. They didn't know much about the banker, but they knew he wasn't good. "Is the banker here?"

"He only came once," Jose Luis said. "He was very kind to me, but he gave me the cider in the teacup. It was the only thing to drink."

Catalina's mind swam. The banker wasn't here, but John had to be, somewhere. She needed to slit his bag. It was the only thing that might undo everything, set things back to rights, heal her brother and Paul. If it didn't . . . she forced the thought away.

"What we need to do is find John," she said. "Where does he go?"

"He's here," Jose Luis said with a shrug. "In the cabin."

"Where?" Catalina gasped, snatching up Pa's knife again from the floor.

"There." Jose Luis nodded to the left. "In the little room where the firewood is. All he does is weep and talk to himself."

Shock riddled Catalina. She looked at Paul again.

"Could be a trap," he said. Then he smiled at Jose Luis. "By the way, I'm Paul."

"Jose Luis," her brother returned, eyes falling on Paul's ax and lighting with interest. "How do you know Catalina?"

"Your sister and I met a few days ago. Or maybe I should say I met her knife."

"What?" Jose Luis's forehead crinkled in confusion and Catalina interrupted.

"If you two don't mind, I'd like to proceed with the plan of undoing a deadly curse. Now, is this where he is?" She pointed to a door next to the bed, and her brother nodded. Warily, she and Paul advanced on it, blades raised once again. The familiar stench of sweat and wood reached Catalina, and her heart raced. She put her hand on the doorknob. Twisted, pulled.

Throwing it open, she and Paul charged inside. Seeds spilled out of the room in a whispery deluge. They were grainy beneath her feet. Jose Luis was right. John was there. He stood against the wall, nose nearly pressed against it, his bag hanging from his shoulder and overflowing with seeds. Muffled moans came from him, and he creaked back and forth like an old tree in the wind. Every few moments, he tried to shuffle forward only to be met with the wall, again and again.

Hesitantly, Catalina approached. The bag hung underneath his arm, protected by his elbow.

"John?" she asked, forcing her voice to be firm. No response. He really did seem gone. Teeth on edge and every nerve heightened in fear, she brushed his arm. It was the first time she'd ever touched him. Coarse angles of bark met her fingers, and it was hard to believe that somewhere inside was a man. John didn't react. Slowly, gently, she turned him around.

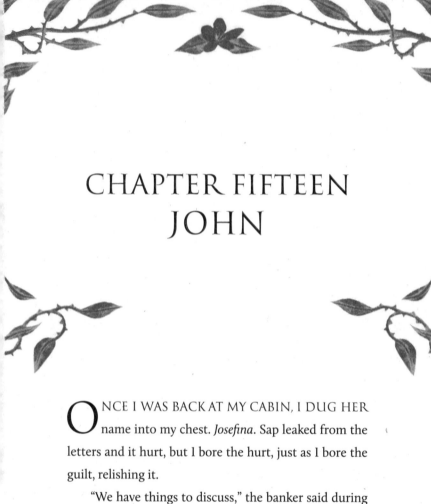

CHAPTER FIFTEEN
JOHN

ONCE I WAS BACK AT MY CABIN, I DUG HER name into my chest. *Josefina.* Sap leaked from the letters and it hurt, but I bore the hurt, just as I bore the guilt, relishing it.

"We have things to discuss," the banker said during his next visit, shortly after Josefina's death. This time, he'd brought a coffeepot to use. Apparently, he wanted bolder coffee than the kettle supplied. He walked toward his usual armchair then stopped. "You've moved them."

Lips pursed, he considered how I'd pushed both armchairs to the side. Tonelessly, I said, "Put them wherever you like."

"I would never. This is your home, Johnny, and if you prefer this lopsided and incongruous arrangement,

I will respect it." He settled into one of the armchairs, but it was obvious the change to his original layout bothered him. I didn't care enough to take any satisfaction in it. "Now, why were you seeking out your son?"

"What does it matter?" I asked. "It ended in disaster. You are well aware."

"I am, true. That bear definitely wasn't my finest work. However, your visit, though unsuccessful, seems to have left an impression. The man—your son—took a trip. Traveled everywhere asking about cursed apple trees. Eventually, he came across a place by one of your orchards and heard of the apple sickness from distraught family members who lost loved ones. Can't say he's fond of you. But that's the way of fathers and sons, isn't it?"

I hung my head. Josefina's name flared bright with pain on my chest.

"Poor fellow. He went to your orchard and saw your apples. They don't call to him, as he is your son, but they happily told him of your horrors and he was shaken to his . . . pardon the pun. Shaken to his core. He was still confused, though. He seemed to wonder if he heard the apples or was imagining it, as they can converse with no one else aside from your immediate child . . . well, no one else alive. But I digress. Why did you go to see him?"

"Just wanted to see them. My family."

Abruptly, the banker struck the arm of his chair with a fist. The unexpected burst of anger startled me. "You forget I know you well, Johnny. Likely better than you know yourself. You would not visit them unless there was a greater reason, one that would outweigh the possibility of harm." The coffeepot hanging over the fire began to boil. Taking a measured breath, the banker got up and poured frothy coffee into one of his teacups. For the first time, he didn't pour me any.

"I wish you would just let me be. Forget me in this Hell and let me rot," I said miserably. I stared at my hand, the one I'd broken off to try to save Josefina. It'd grown back but the crack was still there, running around it like a shackle next to Marguerite's ribbon.

"Really? You'd prefer to never see daylight again?" I'd never seen the banker look surprised before and it was as unnatural as seeing a dog with wings. He quickly took another sip of coffee and when he lowered it, he'd contained himself. "Humans," he muttered to himself. "So loathsomely irrepressible and hopelessly noble.

"But you fail to remember how delightful you are to me, how much pleasure your planting brings me. Now, you must never try to break your curse again."

"Understood. Never again." Already, though, my mind was racing. I put my hand over the name on my chest. For Marguerite and Josefina and Gabriel and my grandchildren, I had to try again, later. But I needed to figure out a solution. People were terrified of me. They would not listen to what I had to say. And Gabriel would be even less likely to, now.

I was so lost in thought I was startled when the banker crossed to me. He grabbed my chin and jerked my head back. Staring into my eyes, he didn't say anything for a long moment. Then, roughly, he released me, picked up the teacup, and threw it onto the floor. Pointy shards of porcelain skittered across the floorboards. Turning back to me, he grabbed me by my shirt, pushed me against the wall, and shouted in my face, "Why do you fight your nature? You are an impoverished boy from nowhere with no one. Stop fighting your curse and embrace it. You can be a monster of legends and yet you keep resisting."

There was nothing to say. Staring back at him, I lifted my chin. I had no soul within my body, but I knew, deep down in the place where it had once been, that I would never surrender to my curse. The banker thought an impoverished boy from nowhere and with no one would give up easily. But maybe that was the thing. When you don't come from anything and you've already ruined everything, what's left might be buried and decay like a corpse in a grave or it might take root and grow into something new like a seed in soil.

"Well then," the banker snarled, still holding me against the wall. "I thought you were broken, but it seems additional pressure needs to be applied and that a punishment is in order. So, listen and hear the end of your hope. I am going to take three of your apples and put them at your son's cabin. Time has passed, and the earth is further ahead. It couldn't be more perfect. The apples don't call to them, but they don't need to. They are starving, now. Winter almost killed them. Your son will eat them. Your grand-daughter will eat them. Your grandson will eat them. I'll poison their water with apple cider too, just to be safe. Your line will be over. Whatever way you thought you might make amends or get them to help you destroy the curse is gone."

"Please," I begged, fraught and panicked. "There's no need. I won't contact them ever again."

"Oh, but you will. I can read it in your eyes as though you were a book. And since I can't trust you, while you are in this cabin waiting to plant, I'll imprison you in your own mind. Gone will be your ability to plot and ponder."

"Imprisoned in my own mind? What does that mean?"

"Have you ever awakened before you awoke?" He spoke slowly. "Found yourself trapped in your own body, mind alive but body dead to your requests? Eyes unable to open, hands unable to lift?" Leaning my head against the wall, I went limp. At my side, the sack was filling again. I put my hand atop it, as though it were a wound I could stanch. "It'll come for you, and the next time you're conscious, your son and grandchildren will be dying at your feet."

The banker had won. He always did. With that, he left. I thought oblivion would descend at once but it came slowly, as though acquainting itself to me. It filled my mind like smoke filling a room with no windows or doors. Wispy at first. Faint, but thickening. I knew it would overtake me before long, so I began to write this document. For you—my family.

As I write now, terror courses through me. I know what is next—that I'll wake beside my son and grandchildren as they die—and everything will be lost. Yet I write, despite it, and I hope, despite it.

CATALINA

Catalina stared into the Man of Sap's face. Tears of sap leaked from underneath lids sealed shut, and his mouth was parted in a moan of perpetual agony. Part of Catalina gave way to the keen edge of fear and the other part wanted to look even closer—to see behind the bizarre monstrosity that had torn her life in two. Anger, confusion, terror, and the tiniest hint of sympathy washed over her. Still staring into his face, she lifted Pa's knife and swiftly brought it toward the seed bag.

John jerked away. His eyes remained shut, but he let out an inhuman wail. Twisting around, he grabbed her by the neck and charged forward. Splintery fingers pressed into her skin. She gasped for air. None came around the relentless grip. He dragged her into the cabin, the wail still emitting.

The red birds burst in through the windows. Glass shattered in lethal bursts of firelit shards. The birds swarmed and ripped at Catalina, Paul, and Jose Luis with their talons, splitting the air with their eardrum-shattering shrieks.

Bright white dots punctuated Catalina's vision and a buzzing filled her ears, making everything sound muffled. Still holding Pa's knife, she tried to hack at John's hand. Bits of wood chipped off, but she couldn't get free or stop him. Paul struck him hard with his ax, and Jose Luis brought a chair down on him. John didn't let go. He tumbled to the floor, dragging Catalina with him in a tussle of leaves and bark. The white dots spread until they became a dense haze between her and the cabin. She fought against it, throat burning in agony and head flooded with a rush of coldness. It was useless, but she still stabbed at John, even as her body slipped away from her command.

Through the dimness, she saw Paul lift his ax and bring it down again, this time trying to sever John's head. At the last moment, John pulled away and Paul's ax bit into the floorboards. She began to drift, the buzzing growing louder and the haze hardening into something opaque, something that would seal her away from the world forever.

Then she saw writing across John's chest. Everything was blurry, but not that. The word seemed to wait for her. *Josefina.* Mamá. Her name was carved deep into bark and the letters bled sap. The sight cut against the haze. Had he killed Mamá? Killed and written her name on his chest like a gravestone? She twisted in his grip, not able to free herself but able to angle away. There. His seed sack flopped on the floor beside them, still hanging from his shoulder, still filling with seeds in its endless task.

Catalina lifted the knife. There was no thought in her mind as she brought it down with strength she should not have had. In one fluid motion, she slashed the blade across the sack.

It slid into the burlap easily, as though it'd been made for that very purpose. A smiling gap spread across the sack. It bulged with seeds then the whole bottom tore away. Seeds flooded out and onto the floor. The sack slipped off John's shoulder as though deflating. Immediately, his grip relaxed and Catalina fell gasping beside him. She dropped the knife and put her hands to her neck, trying to suck in air through aching lungs. John rose to his feet. Paul grabbed her and yanked her away from him.

But there was no need.

Bark shed from John like a snakeskin. Spurts of sap burst from his eyes, then dwindled to a steady trickle, then to nothing. The green leaves turned brittle and dry and drifted to the floor. His birds quieted and settled around him. Just as they did when Catalina took a bite of the apple, they began to sing their mournful death song. This time, though, it was louder with wrenching notes of sorrow. A face emerged, pressing through the bark, and becoming itself once again. Eyes blinked dully, sap still clinging to the lashes in amber beads, and lips quivered, unbound from the heavy cast they wore for so long.

And then consciousness slid into John's eyes. Focus. Awareness. He looked at Catalina, trembling as he touched his shoulder. A flowering shape of redness bloomed beneath his shirt, right where the sack had hung. He moved his shirt aside. There was a giant cavity cut into his shoulder and chest. Layers of pink muscle were gouged aside to reveal white bone. Blood welled in the cavity like an underground spring bursting through the ground. There was no way a person could sustain such an injury and live.

John looked back at Catalina. He was young, she realized, not much older than her. She thought he might be happy to be free from the curse, yet there was only a thick air of guilt upon him, drawing his head and shoulders down as though his body held the heavy record of his wrongs. As though the weight grew too much to bear, he slunk to his knees and bowed his head. His unkempt hair spilled over his face, reminding her strangely of Pa and Jose Luis. Thoughtlessly, she reached out to touch his head, then snatched her hand back.

There were many questions to ask and accusations to fling. The first one came fiery off her tongue.

"Why do you have *Josefina* written on your chest?"

Lifting his head, he stared up at her. Then his head swiveled about as though he'd felt a draft or change in the air.

"He's behind you," he said.

Catalina turned. A man stood by the fireplace, next to Jose Luis. He wore a striking three-piece suit and, in one hand, held a teacup that smelled like coffee. Steam rose from it, and he was careful to hold the handle, not the cup itself. The other hand rested gently on Jose Luis's shoulder.

"Who are you?" Catalina demanded. "Don't touch my brother."

She crossed the room to him, about to pull Jose Luis away. With agile grace, the man moved Jose Luis to the side and his hand went to her brother's neck.

"No need to fuss," he said. He paused to blow across the hot liquid. It made the steam quiver and bend, as though animating with the fear Catalina felt. "I'm the banker."

"You started this." Anger and accusation turned her words into hisses. "You're the one who cursed John."

The banker pushed Jose Luis behind him and came to Catalina, stopping so near that her skirt brushed his shoes. Courage gave way inside her, replaced by a fear that was primal in its weakness and sudden in its inexplicable fascination. The banker was dreadfully stunning, and his features tugged at Catalina's mind, as though what she saw was only half an image. Bizarrely, she could imagine him with wings arching from his back or a crown sitting tilted on his head. Rich notes of bergamot, lavender, and cinnamon emanated from him in the way sweetness wafts off a flower, as though the scent originated from him and wasn't something he simply wore. He made her want to run away, as fast as she could, or move in and bite his lip—anything but simply stand before him.

"Maybe I did." Leisurely, his gaze ran over her then returned to his teacup. He put a fingertip against the teacup's side, its temperature seemingly much more interesting than she. "You seem to already hate me. At least give me a chance to explain. You fail to understand. I give the world to itself. I don't put darkness into the hearts of men. It's already there. Alive, coiled, waiting to strike. All I do is bring it out. Allow it to be, instead of stomping it out."

"Allow it to be?" Catalina spat. "John's apples have killed thousands!"

The banker seemed to weigh her words and shook his head, like he'd found them lacking merit. "Maybe you are seeing it wrong. Evil can have its own meaning, its own worth." He turned to John. "Do you remember the first girl who ate your apples? Do you remember what she said as she died?"

John stared down at the floor and nodded. He mumbled, "How could I ever forget. The poor thing asked for her mother."

"Yes sir, indeed." The banker flashed a satisfied smile. "Now, just wait a minute before everyone makes assumptions. I'm certain you small-minded humans think the child was taken from her mother. It wasn't the case. They were reunited that very day because the woman had already passed before her. What was I to do? When a little girl asks for her mother, only a monster would keep them apart."

The banker looked expectantly around and then frowned when no one was impressed. He tried the coffee, but it was still too hot. With impatient quickness, he set it on the mantel, sighed through his teeth, and raised his hands. The motion was detached, almost like the absent scratching of an itch. The acrid scent of burning wet wood wafted over them. Smoke, coming from his fingertips, floated from his hands and obscured the banker from waist to head. He was reduced to hands and legs extending outward, limbs emerging from nothingness. The smoke cleared and the banker cupped something in his hands.

A tiny lizard, Catalina thought. Yet that wasn't it, not exactly. It was like a lizard in most aspects except for two bony prongs growing from its forehead. The prongs stabbed into its own chest. The only sign of life was its eyes. They blinked in painful misery as blood drained from the fatal wound.

"Ah, my poor child." With the utmost care, the banker crouched and eased the lizard onto the floor. John's birds had been silent, but one of them swooped over and snapped up the lizard. It didn't even open its mouth to cry out. It simply twitched and was still. It'd had no one to defend it, no one who valued it. To the banker, it was nothing, a microscopic footnote against the rage of the world.

Catalina fearfully thought that she and the others likely were as well.

"The birds that attacked us . . ." She thought of their white eyes and teeth-covered beaks. She could still hear their harrowing shrieks as they slaughtered themselves. "Those were your birds, weren't they? You made them."

The banker's mouth twitched as though she'd brought up a sore point. "I did. Difficult things. Ate each other. They were meant to stop you from finding John, but my creations can be a bit unpredictable."

There was a clatter. John toppled over. Catalina turned and her hand went to her mouth. The blood welling across his chest wound was an untamed gush. It poured from the cavity and sank into the floorboards beneath him, a silhouette painted in blackish red. Red and blue veins gnarled across his face like tangled embroidery threads.

"No. Wait." Catalina knelt beside him, realizing she had no answers for who he was or why he had done this to them. If he died, she would never know. Shaking fingers floundered out and she grabbed his hand. A hundred scars covered it as though whatever happened to his bark happened to his skin as well, a story of inerasable hurts. Scars circled his wrist and she realized one of them had to be from her, when she had cut off his hand. Tied around it, below the scars, was a ribbon. It was tattered and stained and impossible to tell what color it had once been.

"It started in a place, long ago," John choked the words out, each one guttural and gasping.

"I don't care about that," Catalina cried. "Tell me why you did this! Tell me why you have Mamá's name on your chest. Why you left apples to kill us and why you took Jose Luis."

A hand grabbed the back of Pa's jacket and threw her roughly aside and a boot slammed down on John's chest. The banker stomped. Lifted his foot. Stomped again. The sounds of cracking bones and squelching organs sickened her, and she knew she would never forget the sounds.

"Stop!" she screamed, but it was too late. The last bit of breath exhaled from John's lips, and he stared at her. Then, just before his eyes emptied of life, his gaze softened, as though he saw someone behind her. He whispered, "Marguerite."

Catalina glanced over her shoulder, but no one was there. When she looked back, John's lids gently closed over his eyes, the livid network of veins receded, and sallowness swept in to limn his face.

The Man of Sap was dead.

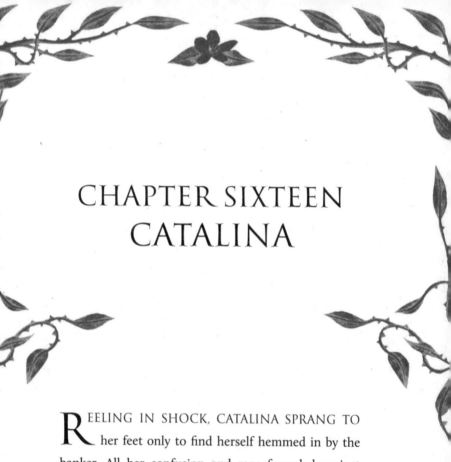

CHAPTER SIXTEEN
CATALINA

REELING IN SHOCK, CATALINA SPRANG TO her feet only to find herself hemmed in by the banker. All her confusion and rage funneled against him, and she struck his chest with both fists. It was like striking stone. Nothing in him gave, not even his clothing. Everything about him was relentless obduracy. With the fierce swiftness of a viper lashing out, he caught her upper arm and held her there.

"Let her go!" Paul surged forward and swung at him, but the banker merely sidestepped and clocked him across the side of the head. He went down, crumpling beside John. Jose Luis charged from behind and the banker caught him by the hair, thrust him into the wood closet, and slammed and locked the door. Though her right arm was immobilized by the banker's grip, Catalina tried to hit him again with her left fist. He simply spun her into him, twisting her right arm behind her back and pinning her other in the crook of his side.

They were perilously close, and he bent her back. He lifted his hand and Catalina cringed, certain he was about to slap her. Instead, he gently brushed her hair back from her forehead. The gesture was gentle yet laced with fire, as though it burned inside his skin and longed to burst out and consume her.

"I deal in secrets," he said, voice tinged with a growl. "You want answers, but they are not yours to have. They died with the Man of Sap. Chasing those answers will be like chasing the wind. You'll always feel the secrets sweeping across your face, but you will never understand them." With one fluidly forceful motion, he turned her outward, so she faced away from him. "Now, let's take an inventory, shall we? You ate an apple but were whisked away to Hell before your soul could leave your body. If I return you to earth, you will finish the process. Your brother and this boy, whoever he is, will too. Slower than you. Small drops of cider take longer to seep in, and your beau is remarkably strong by nature. But it's happening. The contamination, in all three of you."

Catalina wilted in the banker's arms. John was freed from his curse, yet they were still dying as they breathed, right here in the cabin. The realization was a knife stab to her heart, the place where she held her most precious hopes, the ones she never spoke of or let herself think about. There was no speaking them now, and there never would be. And who was she to say *no* when people died all the time and didn't want to? Yet her mind writhed against reality, beating in time with her heart, holding the two names that meant the most to her. *Jose Luis. Paul.*

"There's an opportunity, though. Your soul is still inside you, and is yours to do with what you will. It's the great mystery every human possesses, one I have yet to understand." His voice dropped an octave, tinged with silk and smoke. "There's much I could do with yours, should you give it to me, and there's much you would gain. Your life and the lives of these two boys. Would you like to make a deal?"

Catalina stared at John's body. His face was suddenly more grotesque to her than it had ever been before. If she said yes, would she become something as horrific as he? Half human, half monster?

"Would I be forced to hurt people like John did? Innocent people?" she asked.

"No," the banker said simply. "I would not ask that of you."

"What would you have me do?"

He released her then, thrusting her forward so she stumbled. Letting the momentum carry her across the floor, she unlatched the door to the wood closet. Jose Luis ran to her. Without even certain as to why, she slipped off Pa's jacket and Mamá's jorongo. She put both onto Jose Luis. He stared at her, shaking his head. She made herself smile reassuringly at him, made herself give him a nod, telling him everything was okay. But inside, she realized this was some sort of goodbye, a handing off of her heirlooms to him. Her instinct told her it was, even though her mind cried *no*. Drawing Jose Luis with her, she staggered over to where Paul lay unconscious and knelt next to him. She took his limp hand in hers.

The banker reached into his pocket and removed a velvet pouch. The fabric caught the firelight, its sumptuous threads radiant, much too fancy a thing for this place. Gently, he opened it and shook something out onto his open palm. A tiny seed lay there. It was shaped like one half of a heart. Green iridescence, the sort seen on a beetle, shone deep inside its black depths.

"I've been looking for someone to plant this," he said. "It's a seed from the Tree of Life. I slipped past Uriel, the angel who guards Eden, long ago and stole it. Infernal thing can't be planted by just anyone, though—it must be planted by someone willing to sacrifice everything for the ones they love. Not quite the usual company I run in. Plant it here with care. The fruit it bears, once eaten, will heal all three of you."

"That's the only thing I have to do?" Catalina asked. Suspicion swept thick over her. There was more. There had to be more.

"I'm a busy man," the banker retorted. "If you don't wish to make a deal, tell me now so I may be on my way. I'll transport you back to earth, where you will die, and your brother and your lover will watch before dying themselves."

"What will the terms be? Will there be some way to terminate it?"

"Certainly. If you wish to terminate the contract, simply come to my bank. That's something I offer freely to everyone. Of course, it isn't easy to find my bank, but why the worry? All I ask is that you plant a seed with care."

"Don't do it, Catalina." Jose Luis's voice was full of pleading. He was the boy who saved a winter mouse; the boy who thought her poems were good simply because she was the one who wrote them; the boy who could understand both her and Pa, and see the good in them both.

And she was the sister who was strong enough to save him, in whatever way she needed to. She stood and faced the banker.

"I accept your terms."

The banker reached into his jacket and procured a sheaf of papers. They smelled like warm vanilla and varnished ink. Her name was written on the top in elegant calligraphy. It curled across the page in knots of flourishes and curlicues. At the bottom was an empty line for her to sign her name. The banker held out a pen. Its nib was already dipped in ink, and it dripped onto the floor in red splatters like wax fleeing its candle.

Catalina took the pen. It was slick and heavy. She signed the line, her hasty handwriting defacing the intricately detailed contract, and thrust the pen and pages back at the banker. Without hesitating, she plucked the seed from his hand. A treacherous smile dashed across the banker's face and he motioned elegantly to the door.

"After you."

In the clearing down below, Catalina knelt and drew her hands through the ground. It was sticky but there was dirt, pebbled and grainy. It made her think of Mamá's grave. How she'd seen the gravedigger upturn the earth to make the narrow hole. Even though she stood on its edge and saw the bottom, she'd imagined it kept going. Burying things, in her experience, took your loved ones and turned them to dust, turned some part of you to dust too.

Once she'd cleared away the thicker chunks, Catalina gently set the seed down and patted the dirt over it.

"Catalina?" Paul called from the door of the cabin. He stared blearily down at her, the banker, and Jose Luis. Leaning heavily on the trunk, he limped down the stairs to join them. "What's happened? What are you doing?"

"It's going to be all right," Catalina said. "I've planted a tree and its fruit will heal us all."

"You made a deal with him?" There wasn't a moment of pause. Paul turned to the banker. "I'll take the deal on her behalf. Whatever you want, I'll do it. Just let her and her brother go."

"It's too late," the banker said. "The deal is finished. Her soul is mine. She signed the contract and planted the seed. It's already begun."

"What's already begun?" Paul demanded.

As if in answer, a thin mist pirouetted around Catalina, wisping up from the place she'd planted the seed. Alarmed, she pulled back. The mist, though, simply settled around her. It grew too thick to see through. She was weightless—and then, a few seconds later, seemingly bodyless. She dissolved, like a spoonful of sugar stirred into a mug of red-hot coffee. The sensation wasn't unpleasant. If anything, it was gentle, as though the force behind it didn't wish to hurt her. It didn't matter. It filled her with a thick and nightmarish terror. Desperately, she tried to move. No limbs were hers to command. She tried to scream. No lungs, throat, or mouth were there. Every impulse, thought, and emotion remained, *she* remained, but no material surrounded her. She was bodyless, a single instance of sentience just . . . floating. The mist gave a soft, contented sigh. Then, slowly, she was put back together. Hands, arms, feet, legs, torso, head, they slipped into place, settling on her like articles of clothing. They were hers again. She could open and close her hands. Twist her head. Kick her feet.

Only something was missing. Her soul. It'd left quietly, without a sound. She couldn't pinpoint the exact moment.

But she knew it was gone. A dreadful sensation filled her chest. It wasn't pain. It was an absence, a gaping one, as though something vitally important, vitally her, was gone forever.

The mist sank back down to the earth and released her. It coiled back into the spot it'd come from. With fearful resolve, she looked down.

A web encased her body. No, not a web . . . *lace*, in the form of a long-sleeve, high-neck black gown. It had a train that sprawled out on the ground behind her and sleeves that climbed up her arms to encircle her palms, hooking around her middle fingers. Weight pulled at her hands. She lifted them, examining them as though they weren't hers. They were, though. They were her hands—the same that had tended Pa through his three dying days and held Jose Luis—but changed. In the place of each fingernail was a talon, thick, pointy, and black.

"You look . . . powerful," Jose Luis said, staring at her in awe.

More differences revealed themselves, haunting discoveries that weren't grotesque yet terrified her. Her hair spilled down her back in a cascade of glorious waves. She walked to one of the glossy apples hanging nearby and picked one. Her reflection stared back, but it wasn't the face she'd seen in windowpanes or ponds for the past seventeen years.

Everything was *more.* Her lips were the same dark red as the apple she held, and her lashes curled dramatically upward. No longer were her eyes brown. Black irises met her gaze, indistinguishable from the pupil. Her lips parted in surprise and revealed brilliantly white teeth.

"Catalina?" Paul came to stand next to her. She stared at him, too stricken to know what to say. Everything had changed and she wasn't certain who she was anymore. She felt the urge to go searching, as though she might find her old self somewhere nearby. Gently, he turned her toward him. His touch was familiar and she closed her eyes, letting it tether her to who she had been. The apple dropped from her hand.

The ground shifted. It swelled, gently at first, and then more and more. The teeth, apples, and bones in the trees oscillated in their spots. The roots bursting through the sky rolled up and down themselves, as though trying to get away but not knowing how.

Catalina grabbed Jose Luis, and Paul wrapped his arms around them both. The banker, face impassive, moved to the edge of the clearing. He crossed his arms, waiting and watching. A tree surged up from where Catalina had planted the seed. Just like the seed, it was a glossy black with lustrous streaks of green shimmering beneath its bark. It swelled upward as though borne on a soaring music note, branches shooting out from its trunk and unfurling like majestic wings. Gold leaves interlaced in an ethereal gauze, crowning the tree in a nimbus, as though it were an angelic spirit. Apple blossoms flowered in a swell of scarlet petals and burst, scattering into the air in a fragrant shower and leaving golden apples in their places. The apples shone on the branches, brilliant beams that were so bright, at first Catalina had to shield her eyes.

The Tree of Life was here.

CHAPTER SEVENTEEN
CATALINA

THE TREE OF LIFE WAS SO BEAUTIFUL IT made Catalina wish to bow or reverence it in some way. The crooked, angry landscape quivered and shrank back from the regal tree, the other trees leaning as far away as they possibly could. Catalina's heart raced. All they needed to do was eat the apples. Then they could go home. She would take off the gown, tie back her hair, and figure out life with her new form. But everything would be well. The thought drove her forward to the tree. Taking a deep breath, she reached for the first apple. She thought she would have to pluck it free, but it came away effortlessly in her hand, as though the tree wanted to share its fruits. Immediately, another apple grew in its place.

"Here." She handed one to Jose Luis and picked another for Paul. Finally, she took one for herself, lifted it, bit. Crisp, pure sweetness, underscored by a bubbly carbonation, rolled across her tongue. It was slightly piquant, laced with notes of cinnamon and cloves, and refreshingly cold, cooling her parched throat in a way nothing else ever had before. When she swallowed, the chill turned to a warmth that spread through her entire body and sent delicious shivers through her. It was the most exquisite thing she'd ever eaten yet also the most comforting. It felt like coming home after a long, hard time away or seeing the face of a loved one you thought you'd never see again.

"Catalina! Look!" Jose Luis's face broke into a grin, and he held out his arm. The blisters on it faded. Their bubbles popped and dwindled. The angry red skin turned soft pink, revealing fresh skin. Catalina hugged him, her heart singing. Over Jose Luis's head, she saw Paul. No longer was his face sunken and his eyes bright with fever. The blue around his lips and fingertips melted away. It was like seeing a man freed from the gallows. Life flooded through him, throwing off the heaviness he'd always worn.

Home. Home was next. With a start, she wondered if she had misunderstood the White Spider tree's vision. Maybe her mind had played a trick on her. Maybe she'd taken a step somewhere along the way that had saved them from it. Maybe she would never understand but that was all right.

Then she noticed something. The mist was back. It slunk outward to form a perimeter around the clearing. She dropped the apple she held, and it rolled just outside the boundary. Fearfully, though she wasn't certain why, she bent to pick it up.

Once her hand reached the ethereal line of vapor, it struck something. Hard. Only nothing was there. Confused, she tried again, more vigorously. Her hand hit the invisible barrier again. This time it hurt.

"Now, now," the banker said. "You agreed to plant the Tree of Life *with* care. How will you care for it if you're anywhere else? This is your home now. You cannot leave it."

Catalina's mind spun and she almost vomited on the black lace dress. She turned in a slow circle, tripping on the train, her eyes taking in the borderline of mist. Her whole life was now reduced to this small plot of earth, the tree with the cabin, the brackish creek? The air grew tight around her, and she threw herself against the line of mist.

It was like hitting a wall.

She was trapped. She couldn't stay here—she didn't even know where *here* was. This was the realm of curses and unreality and fear. Panic rose, the same panic she'd seen in bears caught in iron traps, mice in the beaks of hawks, moose surrounded by wolves.

Turning to the banker, she cried, "No! I didn't agree to this."

"But you did. The contract clearly states you will plant the seed with care. So you must care for it. Guard it. It is the Tree of Life. Others will want its fruit. They'll want its healing gifts." The banker spoke casually. "You must stop them. If you don't—if one single other person eats from the tree—you will violate your contract and find yourself not in John's Hell but in one made specially for you, and I'll personally track down your brother and lover and kill them."

"No." Terror almost made Catalina unable to speak. "You said I wouldn't have to hurt anyone."

"I said anyone innocent. Those desperate enough to find their way down here to steal the fruit are hardly innocent. But everything works together. Anyone who is, ahem, terminated, must be buried here. The ground here is hardly fertile. It needs a little help. Their decaying bodies will provide carbon and nutrients for it and, in turn, will make a hospitable place for the tree to thrive. But think of all the time you'll have to write your poems." The banker reached into his pocket and procured a chintz-patterned teacup. He waved his hand over it. It filled with steaming liquid, but it wasn't coffee. Frowning, he turned it over and mud slopped out onto the ground. He tried again and this time cockroaches with stingers crawled from the rim and climbed up his arm. With a snarl of annoyance, he set the teacup down again, shook them off, and muttered, "It's so hard to get a good cup of coffee around here."

Then he faced Catalina, Paul, and Jose Luis.

"It's time for them to go," he said dryly. He waved his hand. Howling wind burst through the clearing like a flash flood tearing through a dry riverbed. It surrounded Paul and Jose Luis. Catalina grabbed for them. Her hand penetrated the wall of wind, but it was like sticking it into fire. She didn't care. She tried to grab them, even as the talons tore off her fingers and the lace tore off her dress. The banker waved his hand again. They were gone. Nothing but emptiness remained.

With a scream, Catalina fell to her knees. Her arm was scraped raw from the wind. White hot pain laced through her hand. New talons emerged in place of the ones torn off. It was a violent regrowth. She screamed again as they ripped through the skin of her nail beds. Blood ran down into the cuffs of her gown.

But that pain was nothing. Not when compared to the realization that Paul and Jose Luis were gone. She would never see them again. And she hadn't even said goodbye.

Turning to the banker, she threw herself at him, clawing at his face and arms. He let her, for a moment, then caught her wrists.

"Calm, little wretch." His eyes bored into hers. "Embrace who you are now."

With force, he threw her to the ground and towered over her. His devious laugh prowled through the air and then he too was gone.

Eventually, Catalina picked herself off the ground and went into the cabin. John's body was limp on the floor. She curled up on the bed, pulling her knees to her chin and her hair over her face. Sobs racked her body until she couldn't sob any longer and she slumped onto her side, body convulsing with tears long expended. She was alone, alone in a way she hadn't known existed, in a way that made her feel like she'd never been born or had already died.

After a long while, Catalina went outside. There was no shovel, so she dug a hole with rocks, tearing the skin from her palms and leaving bloody handprints on the rocks until it was finally done. Then she dragged John's body down the cabin stairs and to the edge of the grave. She rolled it into the pit and refilled it. Task done, she collapsed again onto the ground.

Everything ached and she could trace some of the pain. Her head, where the bride had struck her, her hands, where the digging had wrecked them, her innumerable cuts and scrapes from the river and traveling. But some of it was untraceable, unconnected to any specific hurt, just there, as formed to her as her own skin. She wasn't sure she could ever get up again.

A soft, gentle hum reached her ears. She looked up. The area around her eyes was so puffy from tears that her vision was narrowed. The Tree of Life sang a sweet melody and one of its branches came to her, caressing her cheek and stroking her hair. For a moment, she fixated on the touch, letting it push away everything else. It reminded her of Mamá, how she would brush her hair. Sometimes Mamá would count the strokes in Spanish and other times list the things they had to do for the day, always saying, "¡Y tendremos un buen día!"

Catalina found strength in the memory and finally took a shuddering breath and dragged herself up and back to the cabin. The bed beckoned, but she didn't let herself collapse into it. Instead, she turned in a slow circle. It was obvious John had been here a long time. Deep gouges covered the floor, walls, and even the ceiling, as though he'd been trying to scratch his way out. Random words were etched alongside the slashes. Directions for watering a young apple tree. Birthday gift ideas for Gabriel. Tips for transplantation. A sheaf of papers revealed sketches of apples and apple trees, drawn in great detail. There were also faces. She stared, recognizing images of Pa, Mamá, and then herself and Jose Luis, but when they were much younger. Mostly there were drawings of a beautiful woman with a bright smile, the name *Marguerite* written beneath them and a sun drawn behind her head.

Blood stained the floor where John died, a shadow turned an orangey russet now that it'd dried. He'd had Mamá's name carved onto his chest and had drawn pictures of them. There was a reason why. What were his last words?

It started in a place, long ago. He'd been about to tell her why he'd plagued them . . . or had he been telling her something else? Lifting her head, she stared at all the different words carved into the walls. Starting at one end of the cabin and working toward the other, she read them. There were so many. After a while, her mind spun, and the room seemed to drift around her. But she kept going. Then she saw it.

Long ago.

It was carved onto the floor. Could it be John hadn't meant a time long ago, but an actual place? This place, here, in the cabin? Tapping it, she realized the floorboard was loose. There was a thin gap of space between it and the others, a gap just big enough to slip her talons into. She pulled, wincing at the pressure to her fingers. The floorboard wasn't secured and it lifted away. Letters were inside. Every one was addressed to her and Jose Luis. Taking them out, she settled onto the bed to read them. Most were faded with age, but the top letter was fresh. It read:

Catalina,

I write this, having just taken your brother, my grandson. He is unconscious and I know when he comes to, I will not be. It was not the plan to take him, but when I was pulled from my oblivion to discover myself next to my son's corpse, it was the only thing I could think to do, to hopefully draw you here. Please know it isn't only for me. It is to rescue you too, because the banker wishes to punish me by killing any descendant who can save me.

In taking Jose Luis, I hope you will come save him and—even if not for me—end this curse to save everyone else from my harvest. Or, maybe he will wake, find my letters, and know what to do by ending the curse himself. I have only time to write this quick note because I am falling into oblivion . . . it'll be upon me in just a few moments. I'll hide this letter with the others in hopes the banker will not find it but that somehow you or Jose Luis will.

When I had longer times of consciousness, I wrote a full account of events so you may understand everything.

Please, granddaughter, forgive me, a sinner

The *r* in *sinner* dwindled away into a loop, as though John had been drifting from consciousness. Mind churning, Catalina read the rest of the letters.

When she got to the part where John killed Mamá, she almost had to stop. The morning before Mamá's death had been ordinary, but Catalina had turned it over in her mind so often it'd become brilliant over time, the memory made shiny and precious in the way rocks are tumbled smooth and bright by a river. It was hard to know if the sheen was added by distance, if all the meaningful moments had actually occurred. Frankly, Catalina didn't care.

Because even if it had been their usual routine of getting ready, breakfast, and morning chores, it was sacred simply for how Mamá always made Catalina feel loved amid life's routines.

She read on, learning the truth of the day and aligning it with her own recollection. After Mamá's funeral, Pa brought Catalina and Jose Luis to the minister's home and begged him to let them stay with his family for a few days. When he returned for them, he wasn't merely upset. He was dazed, disturbed. It was then, Catalina realized, that he started telling them stories about the Man of Sap.

Every letter painted her life anew with strokes she hadn't known existed. So this was the reason everything had been torn asunder. John's curse overflowed like his seed sack. It'd consumed his life and then, death by death, it'd consumed hers. The thought filled her with rage, and she lifted her hands and screamed into the silence. When the scream finally died on her lips, she picked up the letters again.

She read them once more. And then once more after that. This time she wasn't looking for answers. She'd gotten those. This time she was looking for hope, a key to the lock of her prison, a map out of the darkness. John said the banker entangled his victims in words. Well, maybe, just maybe, she could use her own words to entangle the banker.

She'd set aside poetry, but words might be the only thing that could save her now.

CHAPTER EIGHTEEN
CATALINA

IT SEEMED FOREVER BEFORE ANYONE FOUND their way to John's Hell. There were no days or nights, so even if Catalina wished to mark the passage of time, it was impossible. It simply *was*, a horror of minutes, hours, and days passing without any method of making them known to her.

Then, on an indecipherable day and at an inde-cipherable time, the trees shivered, and a man slipped warily into the clearing. His clothes were tattered, and he clutched a pistol. Fear made him as jerky as a mari-onette but once he saw the tree, he fell to his knees. Happiness and relief eased the hard set of his jaw and shoulders, and he kissed a pendant around his neck. Catalina watched. She had to stop him. If he plucked an apple from the tree, it would be over.

She stepped onto the top stair.

"Stop!" she called. "Go home."

Startled, he lurched to his feet.

"Who the hell are you?" He squinted at her, pointing the pistol at her.

"Go home," she said again. "Go home or I will have to kill you."

"Can't. My daughter needs one of these apples. I've crossed many lines to get here. Don't think I won't shoot you, girl, because I will. Let me take one. Please. I only need one."

"Can't," she said, and silence fell hard upon them. The man's eyes flickered with fear and then resolve turned them into silvery flints. Catalina knew, then, that only one of them would prevail and the other would be dead. She knew it because the man wasn't seeing her. The determination in his eyes was from seeing someone else in his mind, and it was the only thing that mattered to him. His daughter. She knew it because just as he saw his daughter, she saw Paul and Jose Luis.

He pulled the trigger.

The crack of the pistol rang through the clearing and a chunk of wood spun off from the doorframe. Slivers of wood fractured through the air around her. He didn't stop to reload. Instead, he sprinted toward the tree. Catalina ran down the stairs. The gown didn't impede her. It flowed around her legs, as though one with her intent. Blood thrummed to her fingers, to her talons, instinctually guiding her. Keen, channeled adrenaline flooded her body in a warm wash, some new part of her awakening. It had to be how a hawk felt when snatching a mouse. Primal. Powerful. Predatory.

As the man cut across the clearing, she intersected him. They collided, so hard that pain jolted all the way to Catalina's spine. They fell to the ground, intertwined. He pulled back his arm to punch her, but she slipped her hand up and sliced his neck with one sharp cut of her talons.

It was a quick death.

Afterward, Catalina vomited. The Tree of Life reached gently toward the man as though it wished to heal him. Its branches curled over his face and when it saw he was dead, they drooped and heaved, as though the tree wept.

"Get away!" Catalina screamed at the tree, face stained with tears, bile, and blood. At that, the tree stretched out a branch to caress her arm. With another scream, she slashed at it. Leaves sheared off as easily as petals from a flower. The branch didn't retreat. It simply bore her wrath. She turned away and wiped her face with her sleeves. Closing her eyes, she saw them once again. Paul. Jose Luis. Then she got to work.

It didn't take long to drag the man to the base of the tree. She looped rope around his waist and tossed the end over one of the lower branches. With all her strength, she hoisted his body high, a macabre flag raised in Hell. The Tree of Life let out a cry. Its branches fluttered in distress. Catalina thought it might cast the body down.

"Please," she whispered hoarsely. She tied off the rope and went to the trunk. Lying her cheek against it, she whispered again, "Please."

The tree fell quiet, and though it didn't resume its hum, it didn't stop her. Something tumbled from the man's pocket. Catalina picked it up and let out a raw gasp. A watch. Hours, once again, returned to her. Snapping it open, she desperately stared into it to see what time it was, but a black-and-white photograph covered the timepiece. A young girl, the spitting image of her father, stared back. The watch dropped from her hands. Then, slowly, she picked it up and took the photograph out.

She carried it to the cabin and returned to her spot on the bed. Putting the photo down in front of her, she stared at it and whispered hoarsely, "Forgive me, a sinner."

Eventually, two other bodies swung in the tree. One was a woman with dark hair tied into a bun secured with an elegant black hair comb. The other was another tall, broad man. He'd told Catalina what he wanted to do to her body once he strangled her. It gave her no guilt to kill him, but it was hard to hoist him into the tree. Finally, she got him up. She stood back and was stricken. The White Spider tree. The vision. Three bodies in a tree. This was what she'd seen. It wasn't her, Jose Luis, and Paul. It was these three, three souls who'd sought apples from the Tree of Life. When she'd touched the White Spider tree and seen the foretelling, she'd wondered what sort of monster could do such a thing.

Little did she know the monster was her.

While Catalina lit a candle in front of the photograph of the daughter and the hair comb from the woman, the big man got nothing. It gave Catalina a vile pleasure to see his body spinning gently from the branches. With everything in her, she wished she had Mamá's poetry book and Pa's spectacles to make an ofrenda for them, even here deep in Hell. Despite the heat, she found herself rubbing her arms, longing for Pa's jacket and the jorongo.

Eventually, she picked up a piece of paper and, just like John, wrote.

Fire flickers across my page,
lines of alternating bright and dark,
and I don't know if it is light to see by
or shadows to steal my thoughts away.
And so I let them meet in my heart,
where I keep my ghosts
and I don't fear the dark
because I've learned it is me.

It was a relief to write the poem, finish it, read its words. Before, she hadn't wanted to face herself but now she couldn't help it. Blood formed deep crescents beneath her fingernails, sank deep into the embroidered lace of her gown, and most of it wasn't hers. As she wrote, she wondered if maybe she'd had it wrong. Maybe poetry wasn't there to let you escape. Maybe it was there when you *couldn't* escape.

Finally, a knock came on the cabin door at two o'clock, according to the pocket watch. Catalina walked to the door and opened it.

"Good afternoon," the banker said. He took her in and, for the first time, an ember of interest sparked in his eyes. "You look beautiful, little wretch."

Catalina glanced at the mirror across the way. Her hair was matted into a swirling nest. The black lace dress was torn away at the shoulders, right hip, and neck. Embroidery unraveled from it. It was marbleized with vomit, dirt, sweat, and blood. She didn't reply. Instead, she tried to focus on what she needed to do.

"May I come in?" he asked. "I think a cup of tea might do you good." A white teacup appeared from his pocket. Without a word, Catalina stepped aside so he could enter. He stirred up the fire, filled the coffeepot with water, and set it over the flame. Glancing around, he settled at the table and put the teacup down along with a tiny gold spoon, bowl of sugar, and vial of milk.

"Interior design doesn't run in the family, does it?" His eyes ran over the unmade bed, pushed away from the window to the darkest corner. Catalina had shoved it there after the first man's death because she didn't deserve the view. "Unruly clan, your family. Which brings me to the reason for my visit. You have done well in preventing anyone from picking an apple from the Tree of Life. But please do tell me why you have not buried the bodies as directed? And why they are currently hanging in my tree like strings from a bonnet?"

"You don't like it?" Catalina asked dryly. "Seems like the sort of monument you'd enjoy."

"I admit. It does stir my soul. But if you recall, burying the bodies strengthens the soil, which in turn strengthens the tree. The stronger the tree, the more souls will be lured to it. And nothing stirs my soul more than that, not even this"—he glanced out the window—"treehouse graveyard aesthetic you've so carefully cultivated. I'm hoping you're simply not good at listening and not that you're intentionally defying my directions."

"Of course. I misunderstood," Catalina said quickly. "Though, while I have you here, I wish to clarify something."

"Certainly."

"If I go to your bank, I can terminate my contract there."

"True, and though I don't intend to dampen your spirits, it's located somewhere far away. I don't just mean in terms of miles. It's the sort of distance a child travels when being born . . . mere inches, yet only at the right time. You will not find it. No one ever has." The coffeepot began to bubble. The banker fetched it with a cloth. Taking out another cup, he poured two cups of tea and gently set one in front of Catalina. It had no handle and was covered in a blue-green glaze. At some point, it had been broken, but its seams were mended with gold. She'd never seen such a beautiful cup. The banker noticed her attention. "I got it from Kyoto."

Holding the cup by the rim, Catalina lifted it to her lips and took a sip. Darjeeling aromatics borne on steam reached her nose. The first sip was richly decadent but marred by the taste of grounds, since the water had been heated in the coffeepot. It made her think of Paul and stale coffee and hoecakes for break-fast. With a sharp clink, she set the cup down. Heartbreak threat-ened to submerge her, but she gripped the edges of her chair, pulling herself back from the brink.

"Will you take a walk with me?" she blurted.

"A walk?" The banker cocked his head.

"A stroll." Clearing her throat, she smiled at him. It was the first time she'd made such an expression since her deal. Dried sweat, blood, and dirt cracked at the edges of her mouth and her chapped lips split at the extension.

"As you wish."

They left the cabin and descended to the clearing. Catalina looped toward the creek. The banker stopped and stared up at the bodies.

"You are lethal, little wretch. The one fellow looks strong enough to throw barrels." Catalina shuddered. The banker slipped his arm around her shoulders and brought a hand to her chin. He tilted her face up. "Don't you like what you see?"

The Tree of Life had curled around the bodies. Each body was cradled by branches, as gently as a newborn child. It didn't matter. The wounds slashed across the throats, gory cuts smeared in fluid. The large man's eyes rolled back in his head. Only the whites were visible. The sight sent a fresh wave of nausea cresting through Catalina. She forced it away and made herself spin around within the confines of the banker's arms so she faced him.

"I do like what I see," she said, staring into his eyes. Startlement crossed his face. She slipped her fingers into his and gripped them tightly, so tightly her talons dug into his flawless skin. Ordinarily, her talons cut the flesh, but no blood welled from the wounds. A darkly delighted grin lifted one side of his mouth and he leaned over her. She pushed him back with all her strength. He let her and took a few strides back. In a second, she closed the distance between them.

"Everything is yours," she said. "The Hell you made for John. The dress I wear. My soul."

"It is. All of it is mine, and it still isn't enough." He reached out to touch her hair, but she slashed at him with her talons and the motion lit his face.

"The trees are yours. The cabin is yours. And the creek. It's yours as well."

"Redundant," he said, another smile contorting his mouth, a smile as shaded as the far side of the moon. "But it is true."

At that, Catalina said, "Look where you stand. It's on the bank of the creek. The bank. *Your bank*, that you made."

All emotion evaporated from the banker. He looked down. It couldn't be denied. Both feet stood firmly on the bank of the creek. His gaze found Catalina again and his eyes filled with a forbidding fire.

"It doesn't count," he snarled.

"No?" Catalina asked. "I think it does. The contract said I must meet you at your bank to terminate the contract. You see, you ensnare people with words and deals and fine print. Now I've caught you."

Methodically, the banker turned in a circle, taking in the creek and the bank. Then his teeth clenched. Smoke came from his hands, but he didn't seem to notice. Creatures wheeled into the air, but he was so agitated that they were small slips of being. Three-headed toads with no mouths. Pink rats with ants streaming out of their ears. Squirrels with fangs.

With an acrimonious cry, he lunged away from the bank, but an image sprang up and held him where he was. It was an office. An intricately carved marble fireplace sat against the wall. Chandeliers dripping in crystals floated overhead, aimless and lethargic, bumping into each other. A mahogany desk sat under a window, next to a cabinet full of mismatched teacups. Paneled walls stretched up as far as the eye could see. Documents were pinned to the walls. Contracts. Their many words darted back and forth across the pages, as though trying to escape their papery prisons. Signatures on each flared in crimson and bled a liquid of the same color. Every contract rattled in place and shook in agony.

The banker strode to stand in the middle of the office. Spite twisted his face, turning it into a composition of rage and hate. He met her gaze and, with great effort, composed himself. Stiffly, he smiled at her, and, with a sweep of his arm, he gestured to the room, as though inviting her to admire it.

"And to think." His voice was faint, as though traveling a great distance to her. "That of all people, it's you who sees my office when you, like your grandfather, have no appreciation for design." Stalking over to the wall, he snatched a contract off. It was hers. Catalina could see her name jittering back and forth across the top. Holding it up, the banker tore it in two. Quakes shook the image, and the banker took a step back, balancing himself. "Well played, little wretch," he said. "Good luck escaping."

Then he and the image disappeared.

CHAPTER NINETEEN
CATALINA

CATALINA THOUGHT THE SHAKING WAS from the bank, but it was coming from the clearing itself, spreading out from the tree holding the cabin aloft. The cabin teetered, then fell to the ground with a crash. The roots dangling from the firmament snapped around with the lash of whips. Great black cloudy fissures cracked through the firmament, matching the ones spiderwebbing across the ground. All around, the trees pitched forward and back while leaves tore off their branches. A crackling sound rang out as one of them split in two, but it didn't break like a tree. It twisted and screeched, tearing open to reveal prongs of metal. Bits flew off, filling the air with steel splinters. Apples tore from branches as though plucked by invisible hands, and the teeth and bones shook loose. John's birds, which had been silent in the trees since his death, shrieked and flew in circles, trying to find an escape. It was futile.

Catalina covered her head with her arms. Hell was collapsing. The ground lurched hard, rippling as though pushed from the inside. It threw her off her feet and hard onto her hip. She cried out in pain. Her hair wound around her face as debris pelted her, burying tiny metal shards in her. It couldn't end like this. Not when she was so close. The ground tilted up. Roots tore through it. She caught one of them and tried to anchor herself, even as terror—as uncontrolled as this realm around her—devoured her. With a scream that came from the pit of her stomach, she reached forward for another root and caught that one too.

Cold, freezing air suddenly blasted over her, obliterating the heat. The ground continued to rise and she looked over her shoulder. A wide, empty chasm opened like jaws below. As John's Hell raised upward, everything began to slide into it, as though they were vegetables on a plate being tipped into a pot. There would be no escape from that. Not ever. Lifting her chin, she saw the ground stripping away from the Tree of Life. It alone remained upright and though the wind blistered and the rubble struck it, it was untouched. In fact, it was *growing*. Up. Toward the firmament.

With another scream, Catalina grappled at the soil with her feet and clawed upward. Her talons ripped and streams of blood made her grip slippery. Every muscle burned and shook, the ligaments stretching and then tearing. A giant hunk of metal whizzed by her head, and she ducked just in time. She could feel its force as it passed over her, as violent as a scythe cutting through wheat.

It fell into the void and there was no sound of it ever hitting bottom. She dragged herself forward. One of the Tree of Life's roots was just in front of her. But as she reached for it, the ground inverted even more, dirt crumbling away. With a final thrust, she launched toward the root and grabbed it just as the cursed forest fell into the chasm.

As John's Hell dissipated, the Tree of Life rose, roots and all, through the air. The bodies of Catalina's victims were still nestled in its branches. She frantically climbed through the roots. Once she reached the trunk, she pulled herself onto a branch. There, she threw herself against the trunk, wrapping her arms around it and clinging to it as tightly as she could. Tears streamed down her face, wrought by the wind and the sheer relief that she was here, alive. Despite the roar of John's Hell being rent apart, she heard the beat of her own heart and, deep inside the tree, the faintest hum.

She didn't know how long the tree rose for, but suddenly, just as she'd been spat out of the wind that had transported her to John's Hell, she was thrown out once again. With an anguished cry, she found herself tumbling across dirt. She came to rest against the base of a tree. For a moment, she lay still, utter shock ringing through her body. Then, slowly, she blinked, and branches came into focus above her head. She recoiled away from the tree she'd landed against, but it was simply a pine tree, silent and still in the forest.

Disorientation swam over her. She clambered to her hands and knees then, unsteadily, to her feet. Her dress had torn even further. Its lining and train dragged behind her in shreds while the front cut above her knees. Both kneecaps were swollen and scraped, but her hands hurt the most. Some of the talons had been torn out at the bed, others were hacked into halves. Slick blood covered her hands like gloves. She felt like a battle-scarred creature come to haunt the woods. Breath faint, she attempted to take a step forward. Her legs almost buckled under her weight, but she was able, precariously, to walk.

There was a flutter in the trees nearby. It was a red bird.

"Don Pedro?" she asked hoarsely, trying to swallow against her dry throat. It was him. He cawed at her and gently flew on ahead. "Wait!"

She stumbled after him, mind rewinding to when she and Paul had tracked him. So much had changed since then. As she staggered forward, she saw tree weepers and smelled their fragrant rain. The Tree of Life must've spit her out close to where she'd been before biting John's apple. It could've been her imagination, but she swore she heard the Hill Gog grumbling somewhere nearby.

Don Pedro led her to a two-story cottage built near a stream. Herbs and blossoms lifted their heads above flower-beds. Delicate vines, budded with trumpet-like heads of morning glories, crawled up the cottage walls. Smoke rose from a white stone chimney in lazy curls. There was a red door with a curved top. It was bordered in the same white stones as the chimney. Activity abounded. Chickens and chicks clucked in a coop and a copper-colored horse peered out from a lean-to. Ducks, geese, and pigs ambled contentedly around. Don Pedro flew to a bird-house and disappeared inside.

"Catalina? Is it really you?" Turning, Catalina stared. Jose Luis stood behind her. There were so many changes she was confused for a moment. His hair was shorter now, neat and trim.

His voice, deeper. And he was taller. In fact, he was taller than her now. How much time had passed while she'd been alone, in John's Hell? Only one detail grounded her. He wore the jorongo. "You're here!"

A boyish grin leapt across his face, and he dropped the pail he held to run to her. His arms flew around her. She knew they did, because she saw them, but she was lost in a fog. All of her seemed stiff and frozen and dead. His voice, though, was warm and her arms, of their own volition, rose. Then she was clinging to him, as tightly as she could, despite the pain. She gripped him with all her might, telling herself that this was real: him, his embrace, his love. Finally, she pulled away to stare at him.

"How . . ." Her voice was a frail husk of itself. "Where . . ."

"We've been here for two years," he said. "It's the spot where we were thrown out once the banker sent us away. Every day, we've sent Don Pedro out to search for you. He goes too."

"He?"

"Paul, of course. No matter what, he searches the woods, looking for you. But you're shivering!" He ducked out of the jorongo and wrapped it around her. It settled on her like a sweet grace from the past and she weakly grasped its edges. "Come inside."

Jose Luis helped her into the cottage. Coziness unfolded inside it. It was the sort of coziness that fills a kitchen after a blackberry pie has just been baked with love and the room is still warm and the pie sits on the windowsill with blackberry juice bubbling through the crust. In the first room, a fire crackled in a river rock hearth and three upholstered armchairs sat next to it, huddled together as though in conversation.

"Sit," Jose Luis said. There was a pump with a faucet and basin near the entry, and he levered it up and down. Water gushed from it. Catalina longed for the water, but something caught her eye. A room, off to the right. She staggered toward it.

The sight drove her breath away. Bookshelves, from the floor to the ceiling, filled the four walls. A rolling ladder on rails angled against the nearest shelf. Books fanned across them, each spine beckoning like a portal to a different world, and a desk, with sheaves of paper and an inkwell, sat in the middle.

"Paul's father died." Jose Luis spoke from the next entry. "He inherited the library and brought it here, for you. So you can read and write your poetry."

There was something else on the desk. Catalina walked over to it. It was a book, burned beyond recognition. Mamá's book. Paul had saved it. Gently, as though it might evaporate or pop like a bubble, she touched the brittle pages.

"Here. Water." Jose Luis came in and set a cup down on the desk. "You're bleeding. Let me get some bandages."

Jose Luis bustled away. He was right. Blood covered Catalina's hands, wrists, cuffs. It stained her face and mixed into her hair, fresh new blood, and old dried blood. Catalina was still bleeding and always would be, long after her wounds healed. Slipped into the bodice of her gown was a photograph of a fatherless daughter, placed next to her heart, carried in the way John carried the name *Josefina*. Curses could be broken, yes, but they left scars. Not simply the sort made from dead flesh, but the sort formed over a nerve, so that an ache is always there, just beneath the skin.

She picked up the cup of water and drained it, noticing Pa's jacket hanging on a hook. She went to it and slipped her hand inside the pocket. Pa's spectacle rims were still there. Taking them out, she carried them to the desk and placed them by the poem book.

The last two lines of her poem came to her.

and I don't fear the dark

because I've learned it is me.

They had felt right in Hell, when she thought she might never be saved, when the world seemed to be a terrible story with only one unhappy ending. They felt right here too, but maybe there was more to the poem. Just maybe.

"Catalina?"

She knew the voice in an instant, but she didn't turn. This place was full of life. Jose Luis teemed with happiness and sunshine. She, though, was a girl abandoned in Hell, who had sold her soul and become a killer.

Perhaps she was the taint now.

Paul walked around to face her. He stared down at her and, slowly, she looked up at him. For a moment, she forgot what he saw and only saw him, her eyes taking in the face she didn't know she'd see again. Messy, overgrown hair fell over his forehead and brushed his collar while a scruff of beard shaded his cheeks. Like Jose Luis, he seemed cut from sunshine. A hint of intimidation passed over his face but then it was gone, as though he willed it away.

"You're here," he rasped, and then "You're home."

His words made something break in Catalina. But not break in a bad way. Break in the way something does when it's held too much weight for much too long—or perhaps has held something it was never meant to hold—and finally gives way to it. With a swift step, she came to him. His arms swooped around her with desperation, as though he wished he could snatch her away. She had to stop him. To tell him what she was.

"I've—you don't know what I've done," she whispered into his shirt.

"I don't give a damn," he whispered back. "And I never will."

"It isn't that simple. I'm changed."

"Catalina. Do you know what I thought when I first saw you?"

"What?" The question was raw on her tongue.

"I thought, 'This girl might kill me.'"

"And now?" She pulled back, making him see her, face her.

"Well, now you might really be able to kill me." He kissed her. Kissed her as though she wasn't covered in salt sweat and old sick, as though she wasn't a girl metamorphosed into a monster, as though she wasn't anything other than someone he loved. A thaw stole into her heart and her numb stupor began to melt. She had changed, it was true. But maybe they, together, were their own creation. Maybe that creation had its own Eden, a place no one could enter or touch but them.

Life was cruel, certainly. It was filled with bright, ravaging horrors that stun you like a sun flare and secret, quiet wounds that fold against your ribs. It took loved ones from your arms so you breathed hurt like air.

But it was also full of mysteries. And there was room in mysteries. Room for things to be different. For them, despite the pain, to be all right.

THE END

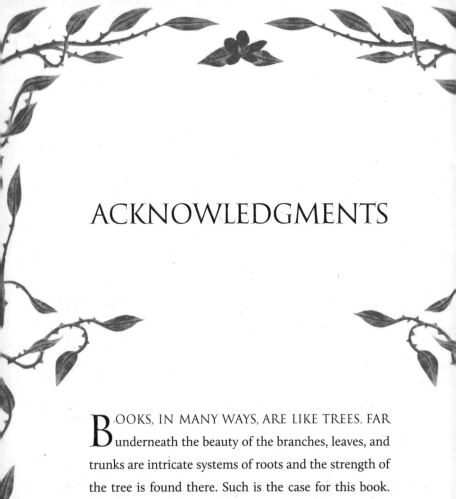

ACKNOWLEDGMENTS

BOOKS, IN MANY WAYS, ARE LIKE TREES. FAR underneath the beauty of the branches, leaves, and trunks are intricate systems of roots and the strength of the tree is found there. Such is the case for this book. So many people have helped it—and me as a writer—to grow and I am so thankful.

First of all, thank you to my agent, Susan Hawk. You took me under your wing as a little weak sapling and have helped me reach my branches toward the sky in so many ways. Thank you for everything you have been to me and how you have helped me reach my dreams.

Thank you to my editor, Ashley Hearn. This tree of a story had very twisted branches until you came along and through your magical forest fae touch straightened it out. Thank you for not only for your writerly wisdom but for the love and encouragement you so freely poured into this book. In many ways, you were its soil, sun, and water. There are certain comments you left in my manuscript that I will never forget and will turn to when this writing journey gets hard.

To my cover artist Michelle Avery Konczyk and cover designer Lily Steele, thank you both for bringing my cover dreams to life in such a darkly decadent and exquisitely eerie way. The apple being eaten will haunt me in the best ways possible forever!

Thank you to Peachtree for giving my book a home in such a wonderful forest of stories and to Penguin Random House for its marketing and distribution. Thank you so much to Nikki Langlois and Lauren Kelsen for the encouragement and help with the street team and pre-order campaign. Also, thank you to Reyna Johnson and Sofía Aguilar for your authenticity reads.

To my writing community, I feel like you are the birds in my branches, singing me songs of hope when I forget how it goes. Christianna Marks, love you forever, write or die always! Katie Bagley, I adore you and am so thankful for your friendship. Jenn Barnes, where would I be without you? Aimee Payne, you are in my heart. Alix Morgan, I'm convinced we are soulmates across continents. Hepzibah Becca Jael, I'm yours till the end of time. Michelle Lynn Villa, you are a true kindred spirit. Amy Shane, I'm so glad I know you. Liz Griffin, you inspire me in so many ways. To the Beautiful Sisters Comeaux, I love you both and thank you for letting me borrow your last name for Marguerite. Jane Vampa, thank you for lending your artistic expertise to me and for working with me to get my little authorial extras just right. Kaela Stager, I so enjoy our writing dates and time together.

Emily Kazmierski, writing beside you is an honor and how fun is it that we get to just talk shop all the time? Em Luethy, thanks for being the glitteriest book president ever! Frankie Munson, may our continuous chat era never end. Thank you for your unwavering belief in me. Jessica Burgos, to all the ballgowns and pretty book covers! Love you! Alex Brazle, thank you for always being such a light. Tatyana Garten, I'll never forget how certain you were this book would sell. To the icons of Instagram and TikTok, huge thanks to Layana Clouet and Pauline Roxas. You two are the best. Gina Riccitelli, so thankful for you, my galaxy-eyed friend. Thank you to Briana Urban for being such a wonderful friend and support. And to my Bookstagram community, thank you so much. I am forever grateful for all of you.

To my street team, I can't thank you enough for supporting this book and helping it find its readers. I am so lucky to have you all.

To my readers, there are no words. Only gratitude.

George Grimaldo, gracias por ayudarme con mi español y por cuidar tan bien de mi Ky!

To my parents, the OG founders of our family tree, thank you for the atypical childhood—honestly! You let me find my words without oversight or interruption and I'm not sure I would've otherwise. Hi Kyyyyyyy yes you're in this book but of course!!! Love you more than life sissssy. Seth Mas, love you and always look forward to our Saturday night hangouts. Leilani, you were there for every draft of this story. Every meltdown (of which there were many). Every rejection. Every revision. Thank you just doesn't feel strong enough. Love you, sister.

To my precious children, who are the flowering branches of my life. Baby girl, you are on your way and due to arrive just around the same time as this book, making this a truly special and unforgettable year. Juliet and Declan, you are my joy and being your mama is one of the best things that has ever happened to me.

Mark, you are the photosynthesis that takes my madness and turns it into something like magic. You are always my way out of the dark woods. Ever mine, ever thine, ever ours.

Thank You to God for making a world with trees. Apples. And stories. I am grateful for this love of writing You put into me and opportunities for my writing to be read. Soli Deo gloria.

ABOUT THE
AUTHOR

AUTUMN KRAUSE is the author of the YA novel *A Dress for the Wicked* (HarperTeen). She received her MFA from VCFA and currently lives in Orange County, California, with her husband and three children, and can most often be found wearing a black lace dress.